The SECRET DIARY of MONA HASAN

The SECRET DIARY of MONA HASAN

Salma Hussain

tundra

Text copyright © 2022 by Salma Hussain
Cover art copyright © 2022 by Jameela Wahlgren

Tundra Books, an imprint of Penguin Random House Canada Young Readers, a division of Penguin Random House of Canada Limited

Library and Archives Canada Cataloguing in Publication

Title: The secret diary of Mona Hasan / Salma Hussain.
Names: Hussain, Salma (Young adult fiction writer), author.
Identifiers: Canadiana (print) 20220143307 | Canadiana (ebook) 20220143315 |
    ISBN 9780735271494 (hardcover) | ISBN 9780735271500 (EPUB)
Classification: LCC PS8615.U929 S43 2022 | DDC jC813/.6—dc23

Published simultaneously in the United States of America by Tundra Books of Northern New York, an imprint of Penguin Random House Canada Young Readers, a division of Penguin Random House of Canada Limited

Library of Congress Control Number: 2022930330

Edited by Lynne Missen
Designed by Sophie Paas-Lang
Printed in Canada

www.penguinrandomhouse.ca

1 2 3 4 5   26 25 24 23 22

Penguin
Random House
tundra | TUNDRA BOOKS

To the dreamers.
And as with everything I do,
to and for the best kids in the world, R & Z.

"Be kind, for everyone you meet
is fighting a hard battle."

—Anonymous
(often misattributed to Plato, and
believed by wise people everywhere)

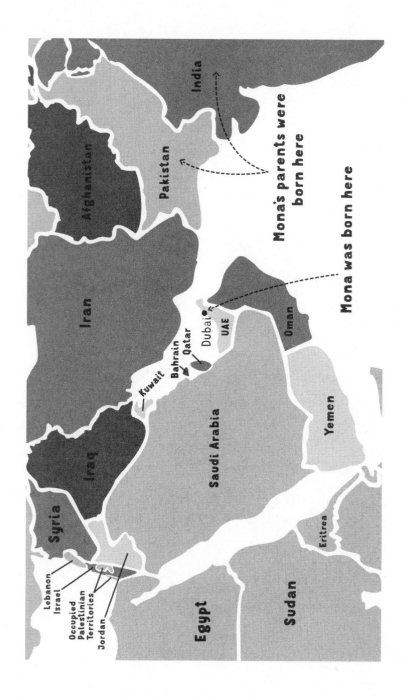

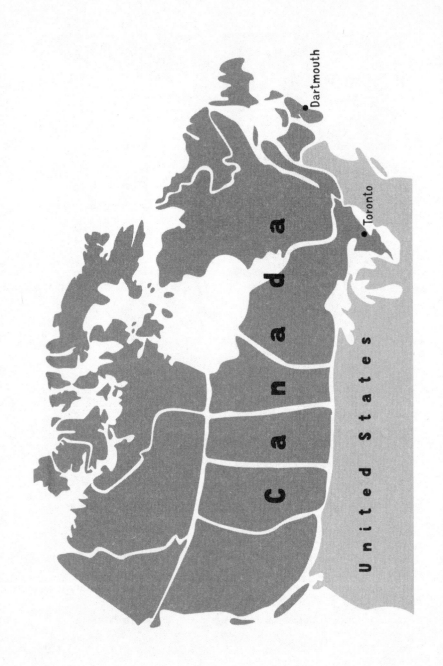

CHAPTER ONE

January

Tuesday, January 1, 1991

Ten minutes past midnight:
My New Year's resolutions:

1. I will save a life from danger!
2. I will not roll my eyes behind my mother's back.
3. I will not roll my eyes behind my father's back.
4. I will make every attempt to get along with my icky little sister, Tutoo.
5. Every night I will put my school uniform in the laundry hamper.
6. Every week I will tidy my room.
7. Occasionally I will make my own lunches for school.

8. Oh, and after hearing from my mother that I received gushing accolades—a-c-c-o-l-a-d-e-s— from all my teachers at the mid-year parent-teacher interview, I also vow to help the dum-dums in my class with their homework.

At our New Year's party tonight, Uncle Annoying brought two bottles of Canadian ice wine for all the grown-ups to try! Tasting exotic new drinks from faraway countries may sound like a fun thing to do for New Year's, but if the Dubai police hear about what we Muslims were up to, we could be done for.

Mid-morning: I woke up exhausted today. It's my parents' fault for throwing fun parties. Just my luck to have parents like them! Before Tutoo and I were shuffled off for bed, we saw all the grown-ups sipping their ice wine daringly from little Turkish coffee cups. There is a chance our parents could become alcoholics. Next year, Tutoo and I could be sent off to the Dubai orphanage.

At the party last night, I heard Aba use the word "sekkular" and talk about a British author with an Indian name. Then in heated, hushed tones, the grown-ups argued about something called "fada" in their tea. When I asked my father how to spell "sekkular," and who Uncle Salman Rushdee is, and what "intifada" is, Aba's eyes bulged until they almost popped out of his head. He promised to explain these things to me when I'm older but in the meantime, he made *ME* promise to never use these words outside the home and rushed me off to bed. *Or else.* Or else stonings and lashings, I suppose.

Tutoo and I overheard other Mystery Words last night and no one would spell those out for us either, so we made a list.

Wednesday, January 2, 1991

Aba went to work today. He works a lot. Ami calls him a "workaholic," and he sometimes chews with his mouth open, so she also calls him "intolerable." I don't know how my mother made it through the holidays.

Aba is a banker and works in a shiny glass building. He moves money for important people and studies numbers. He works long hours, and the bank pays him a lot of money. When Tutoo asked why they give him so much money just to look at numbers all day, he explained, "No one would do this job otherwise. It's not like being a teacher or an artist. Those folks would do their jobs for free." Ha! My father doesn't know half the teachers at our school. They are always shuffling around moaning, "They don't pay me enough for this."

Thursday, January 3, 1991

Laila came round in the evening. She had a tan from spending her holidays in the south of Egypt. My mother scolded her for her time under the sun: "Chee chee, Laila! How could you let this happen? When your tan comes off in a few weeks, you can go back to being pretty." Laila is my best friend and Egyptian, but the funny thing is that with her darker winter tan, she is now the same shade of Pakistani-brown as I regularly am, year-round. Tan or no tan, I noticed that Laila's breasts looked bigger. Not that I was ogling them, just eyeing them discreetly to compare.

While listening to Madonna's Greatest Hits from the Greatest Era Ever (the 1980s, of course), I jammed the cassette player by losing a charm from my bracelet inside. Now it's not closing properly. Nobody knows yet, and with a bit of luck, everyone will think Tutoo did it. I will be glad to get back to school soon.

Friday, January 4, 1991

Ami, Tutoo and I went to Al Ghurair mall to check out the new fashion trends and fads. This futuristic decade is all about BRIGHT COLORS and CONTRASTING SCHEMES. Satin dresses with black leather boots. Ripped jeans with cashmere tops. Plaid shirts with denim collars. And fluorescent colors on everything so that it looks like everyone just stepped out of a comic book. It seems that OLD-FASHIONED patterns are OUT and EXPERI-MENTATION is IN!

I wear a uniform at my private school every single week-day from Saturday to Thursday, but on Fridays, I'm free to wear whatever I want. That's because Fridays are Holy days and school is closed. On Holy days, our family rushes through prayers, then we go jumping in the waves at the beach, eat roadside shawarma, slurp mint lemonade and end the night with pistachio ice cream.

I've decided that to keep up with this futuristic era, I'm also going to experiment with my fashion choices, which is why I bought shiny gold tights, a shredded T-shirt with thunderbolts on it, two lace chokers, three mood rings and a pack of neon-colored scrunchies! Oh, and extra-hold hair-spray to tease my curly bangs higher, of course. Watch out, World, here comes Mona Hasan, age eleven and nine weeks!!

Saturday, January 5, 1991

Tomorrow is the first school day of the new year, and I can't wait to go back to the second half of sixth grade! The December break was a MAJOR SNOOZE-FEST. Other than the beach on Fridays, and excursions to the closest mall on weekdays, Tutoo and I spent most of our holidays inside our air-conditioned ~~cage~~ apartment fighting each other for the remote control. Just our luck to be stuck in the most boring city on earth! Nothing exciting ever happens in our corner of the world.

Sunday, January 6, 1991

OLD IS GOLD, BUT NEW IS BOLD!

At the morning assembly, we found out that we have a brand-new principal this year—Mr. Qadri. Mr. Qadri sang along to the UAE national anthem, then he gave a short speech afterwards. He said he's "honored" to be our new principal and is looking forward to getting to know all of us! What kind of man principal wants to know his girl students?! We had to hold back our snickers.

Mr. Qadri also announced his first rule change. He wants the girls to use the gymnasium for PT class and learn actual sports! No more running around the field playing tag.

Mr. Qadri spent ten long minutes giving a lecture about how playing sports would make our brains stronger and faster. Ha! Little does he know that my brain is already strong and fast, and what I'm really hoping for is that sports will make my chest bigger and rounder!

I heard the teachers grumbling about the rule change. Not only is the gymnasium in the boys' section, meaning a long walk across the hot field for all of us, but now our PT teacher, Mrs. Naz, will have to spend the class actually talking to us. As far back as I can remember, Mrs. Naz has spent

PT class standing under the awning drinking a can of Fanta. Whenever she sees any of us on the verge of dehydration, she blows on her whistle to send us indoors.

Monday, January 7, 1991

A new girl in our class!!

Her name's Maryam. She's pretty, for sure. She has the kind of face that you just want to stare at for as long as possible. But the problem is that she knows it.

She's moved here from the UAE's capital city, Abu Dhabi, where she was at a prestigious co-ed *American* school. Rumor has it that she was the top student there. Her hand shot up for ALL the toughest math questions. Straight and fast. She had a fancy pencil case with lots of little buttons. All her pencils were neatly sharpened and her shoes were spit-spat polished and scruff-free.

At lunchtime she came up to Laila and me and sat with us under the date tree. We smelled her before we saw her. A cloud of vanilla and cinnamon wafted from her. New Girl smelled lovely. We smiled up at her hopefully. She was so shiny and perfect. I held my breath as she seated herself next to us. She unclasped her tin lunchbox. Her food was neatly organized in smaller containers. Slices of mango. Salted disks of cucumber. Fragrant kofta. Garlicky hummus. Za'atar bread cut into neat triangles. Oh man, she even had a perfect mother, didn't she?

She looked over at us. Laila slid her container with the stuffed grape vines under her skirt. I wolfed down my aloo paratha so fast that I started hiccupping. I shot the new girl, Maryam, a wide, gummy smile. That's when she looked down at our legs. "Oh, you're both Half Socks." She sighed. Gathered her stuff and left. She found a group of girls wearing tights that covered their whole legs, the "Full Socks."

Every few months, our class divides into groups—the Hindus stick with the Hindus, the Coptic Christians with the Coptic Christians, the Sunnis with the Sunnis, the Shias with the Shias, and so on. But after a few weeks, if there haven't been any major religious festivals or holidays, everyone forgets and divides *again* into groups for other, far more important reasons. Groups for the ones who ace their tests and the ones who don't. The ones with pierced holes in their ears and the ones without. The ones who mostly watch Hollywood and the ones who mostly watch Bollywood. This time around, the groupings are the girls who wear socks to their knees (the Half Socks) and the ones who don't (the Full Socks).

Laila and I spent the rest of our lunch hour bemoaning our mothers, who seemed dead set on ruining our lives by not buying us full socks.

Tuesday, January 8, 1991

Today we were supposed to have our first gym class ever, and I was so excited to learn about new chest-growing sports, but alas, we are off to a very bad start! Our whole class had to spend the morning standing at our desks and our much-anticipated first gym class ever has now been moved to next week! Someone wrote "SPORTS ARE FOR SLUTS" on one of the washroom stalls, and PT class was cancelled. *SLUT* was underlined three times in thick, angry ~~lashings~~ lines.

"Who wrote this word?" our homeroom teacher, Mrs. Adila, demanded all morning. No one looked up.

"What does this word mean?" we asked each other at lunchtime. No one could find it in any dictionary, so it's clearly misspelled.

Thursday, January 10, 1991

Uncle Annoying dropped by today with his wife and their newborn baby. Uncle Annoying is Aba's friend from work, and we haven't seen him since the New Year's party. Ami and Uncle Annoying's wife disappeared into the kitchen, and Aba went downstairs to fetch a new copy of the newspaper, as he'd spilled coffee on the one from this morning. Uncle Annoying took everyone's absence as his cue to play an annoying game where he chased Tutoo and I around the living room, grabbed us from behind and started tickling us. We are much too old for this game, so I came up with an escape plan pretty quickly—with my thumb and pointer finger, I latched onto a single one of his arm hairs and yanked, dead sudden and hard. He dropped me like a hot potato after that. Poor Tutoo had to struggle for longer.

When our parents were back and gathered in the living room again, they dove into a discussion of the headlines in this week's newspapers—"Iraqi President Promises 'Mother of All Battles'" and "9 Injured in Border State Bomb Blast" and "Truce in Hot Spot Region Under Threat—*Again*."

Nothing exciting ever happens in the UAE, but there *is* bad news happening all around us. There's lots of fighting going on and the latest ones to enter the boxing ring are Iraq and Kuwait. They started fighting last summer and are *still* at it this year! Because of their fighting, satellite dishes have popped up everywhere and we now have a new American TV channel showing us the bad news nonstop. This new channel's motto seems to be "Why worry *later* when you can worry *right now?*" All the grown-ups in the UAE watch the news and read three different newspapers in two different languages every day. Everyone wants to know: Is the bad news moving closer?

In the back pages of today's *Gulf News*, I noticed a box with a thick black border, a pointy leaf and an announcement in rhyme:

WANT OLD-AGE PENSION AND
FREE HEALTH CARE?
OCEANS, MOUNTAINS AND FRESH AIR?

THEN CALL CANADA'S TOP
IMMIGRATION EXPERTS,
MR. SHARMA & ASSOCIATES, TODAY!
MAKE HASTE AND DO NOT DELAY.

Friday, January 11, 1991

Ami went for a driving test this morning but failed it (again!). She has been banging the pots and pans in the kitchen ever since.

Every year Ami takes the driving test, and every year the examiners at the Dubai Roads and Transport Authority fail her. There's a mystery number of women who can get driver's licenses in Dubai each year—only that mystery number and no more. Either she hasn't been lucky yet, or she hasn't found the right person to bribe yet. When I eavesdropped on her phone calls, I heard Ami tell her auntie friends that she does not like the people working at the Dubai Roads and Transport Authority. She even used swear words in two different languages! Mortification to the nth degree. She is not like the mothers on TV.

Saturday, January 12, 1991

My mother said she found a word in my dictionary that describes herself. It is *captive*. When Tutoo and I got home from school, she was still in bed bad-mouthing the driver's license examiners.

I wish my mother had a driver's license like Laila's mom so that my mother could have someplace to go every day when all of us go to work or school. If my mother had a license, then she could even have a job like Laila's mom. My mom could be a teacher like Laila's mom. Well, actually, mothers can *only* be teachers. Aba is a banker, and only fathers can be bankers. I tried to explain this to Tutoo, but of course eight-year-old baby sisters don't understand anything about anything.

I was three when Tutoo was born, but I still remember the afternoon when Ami came back from the hospital and put her on my lap. Ami says that during this time, Aba was "pulling himself up by the bootstraps like all the other ajnabis or foreigners in the UAE." He had grown up "dirt-poor" in Pakistan and borrowed money to take a one-way flight from there to Dubai in search of the Great Expat Life. He took a bottom position at one of the big banks and worked his way up. The early years were dead rough. We lived in a cramped two-bedroom in Dubai's poorest neighborhood, Karama. No elevators. No marble floors. Not even a bidet! And just one TV!!! I don't know how we made it through those tough times, Allah!

That afternoon in Karama when baby Tutoo was thrust into my life, she peed on my lap, then started wailing. Ami rushed over to soothe her. That was the exact moment I understood that for the rest of my life, my little baby sister was going to be a STINKY, ICKY ATTENTION-HOGGER. Both Ami and Aba work so hard to treat us equally and they just won't admit that I'm their better child. It's terrible.

Sunday, January 13, 1991

Ami invited three of her friends to come over. They arrived after school and Ami greeted them at the door with, "Welcome, fellow perfumed captives."

The aunties brought their army of brats with them, and Ami shepherded them into MY bedroom. As I was the oldest in the group, the aunties asked me to watch over them and make sure that they didn't stick Lego pieces up their noses. Then they went to feast on all the goodies in the living room and talk about a book called *The Female Yoonuhk* by some German writer. Us kids only got a go at the goodies after the mothers had eaten first. The tyranny—t-y-r-a-n-n-y!

I gave the toddlers a long lecture about not touching anything in my bedroom, then I told Tutoo to be a big girl and watch them so I could go hide in the hallway and eavesdrop on our mothers. I missed their discussion on the book, but I did hear them gossip about the other mothers at school, reminisce about their childhoods and share naughty jokes with each other. Out of all the mothers, MY mother was laughing the loudest and the most often. Ugh, she is almost thirty-one! I wish she would act her age.

Monday, January 14, 1991

Ami said she found another word in the dictionary that describes her—*feminist*. Feminist is one of those words that makes you go cavorting around the dictionary to find out what it means! In the dictionary, its definition is "of or relating to feminism." And *feminism* means "a range of social and political movements and ideologies that share a common goal: to define, establish and achieve the political, economic, personal and social equality of all genders." But what is *range* and what are *ideologies* and how would you *establish* an idea, and what exactly is *social equality*? It will take me forever to understand any of this. *YAWN!* Obviously the smarter (and faster) way for me to figure out what feminist means is to watch more movies and thumb through more women's magazines.

I don't always fully understand what the grown-ups are saying because they speak with so many Mystery Words. Or if they want to be super secretive, they use our "mother tongues"—Urdu or Hindi or Arabic. The languages *they* grew up with but not the ones they want *us* growing up with. I think and dream and hope only in English. This is because I'm in Dubai's best English-medium school, the esteemed "Sheikha Khalidiya bin Latifa Al Nahyan British English All-Girls International Islamic Institute for Academic Excellence." Sure, it's a mouthful, but the name needs to be super long to explain that it's an international and Islamic and English school all jumbled up together.

Of course, I can speak in Urdu if I want to (theek thaak) and in Arabic if I need to (shway shway)—but my parents want Tutoo and I to focus on the English part: They want us to read books *mostly* in English, listen to music *mostly* in English and watch movies *mostly* in English. Our parents make an exception for the one Bollywood movie featuring a mixture of Urdu and Hindi that's shown every Thursday night on Channel 33, which they sit down and enjoy with us too. Aba says that the Bollywood movies on Channel 33 are our "weekly diversion from the tyranny of our realities." I haven't a clue what he means by that! All I know is that the movies come with English and Arabic subtitles, so most of Dubai makes an exception and tunes in too.

Laila's parents have the same "mostly English" rule for Laila and her brothers. The only Arabic they are encouraged to listen to is from Oum Kalthoum songs. In fact, everyone my age has this same type of rule, even if their parents don't speak English well. Sometimes *especially* if their parents don't speak English well.

Tuesday, January 15, 1991

First PT class and I counted 786 steps across the scorching field to the boys' building. Inside the AC blasted frosty air. The floors were shiny and the walls looked freshly painted.

Mrs. Naz taught us "basketball"—a dead difficult game with a *LOT* of rules! When nothing else is on, I've watched this game on TV, but I've never understood how it works and I've definitely never played it before! The important rules we learned today were that to move the ball, you had to bounce it on the floor with one hand, but when you wanted to pass it to someone else or throw it into the ring on the wall, you could use both hands. *Confusing!*

Mrs. Naz read off more confusing rules about where to stand to score points—one point for "foul shots," or two or three points for "jump shots," "layups" or "dunks." But the problem was that none of us could score *any* points at all. No matter where we stood, none of us could get that heavy ball into the high goalpost! Not even Mrs. Naz! Is that metal ring even big enough to fit the ball?

It was such a difficult sport that we ended up playing tag on the gymnasium floor instead. Mrs. Naz said we would try a different sport next week. So much for bigger bongos— all I had at the end of class were aching shoulders! I asked Mrs. Naz if I could be excused from PT tomorrow. All that messing around with passing and taking turns is a sheer waste of time. Mrs. Naz replied, "Mona, the purpose of school sports is to develop a character of camaraderie and collaboration, and you, of all the girls in this school, need to develop these traits as a matter of urgency." Grown-up mumbo jumbo! I'll have to ask my mother for a note to excuse me from PT instead.

Wednesday, January 16, 1991

I woke up with a bit of a cough this morning, so I asked Ami for a note to excuse me from PT class. She said she refused to mollycoddle me a day longer! The indignity! I've never seen any grown woman jogging out in public, and now I understand why. How would Ami like to run wild and free under a desert sky? Chee chee! Sweating in front of others is no way to live! Anyway, my mother is sorry now. Mrs. Naz kept us out on the open field for the whole hour and I came home with a tan.

After all the jogging, Mrs. Naz taught us the rules for "softball." The ball was definitely *not* soft! We kept getting confused about who was supposed to catch the ball and who was supposed to run to the base. Halfway through the game, I smashed into someone from the other team—we were both trying to catch the ball, even though we were on opposite teams. Mrs. Naz blew on her whistle, and we took a break to get ice for the bumps on our foreheads. Thankfully, that was the end of that! For the rest of class, we played a game of tag out on the field. I hope next week we go back to sports that have to be played inside the boys' air-conditioned gymnasium.

Before bed I surveyed my chest again. Am dead worried. Laila's cha-chas are coming along nicely, and she even said her mother is taking her bra shopping next week. Just my luck.

Friday, January 18, 1991

Ami unplugged the TV and hid the remote this morning. Before doing so, Tutoo and I heard that Iraq's president shot "scud—s-c-u-d—missiles" into Tel Aviv and Haifa last night. Twelve people died. All of Dubai's newscasters are wondering, "Will Tel Aviv insist on retaliation?" There were a lot of other big, fancy words, and there was lots of talking in circles by important TV people and politicians, but there were no answers.

"That's a dirty word—don't give it more attention," Ami told me when she saw me looking it up in the dictionary. After Ami left the room, I winked at Tutoo, pulled the cap off my marker and wrote *retaliation*—r-e-t-a-l-i-a-t-i-o-n— on the inside of my arm. Tutoo stared up at me and asked, awestruck, "You know how to spell all the big, fancy words, don't you, Baji?" I replied to my simple sibling in my sophisticated Big Sister voice, "Tutoo, of course I do. When you're eleven turning twelve, you know *everything* about *everything*."

But when Ami walked back into the room, I pressed my arm against my body so that she wouldn't see what I had transcribed from the dictionary and pull my ears for it. Ami gave us a lecture about ignoring the stupidity on TV. Then she lathered my face with a homemade turmeric and chickpea flour paste to lighten my tan. "Stay out of the sun if you want to be one of the pretty girls," she chided.

Saturday, January 19, 1991

Mr. Qadri summoned the whole school for an assembly this morning. Even the teachers who like to hide out in the air-conditioned staff room were forced to attend.

When the school was lined up in rows, Mr. Qadri cleared his throat into the mic. Then he began, "As-salamu alaikum, everyone! Today is . . ."

SCREEEEEEEEECH!

A high-pitched squeal erupted from the mic. Most of us covered our ears. The teachers winced. Mr. Qadri waited until the noise settled, then he continued. "Today is a day that will go down in history. A monumental moment for the Middle East! Operation Desert Storm has officially been announced." He explained that the announcement meant that America's military were arriving next month to sort out the argument between Iraq and Kuwait—the much-anticipated "ground offensive"! Boots on the ground. Actual soldiers! We instantly felt relieved, as we all know from listening to the politicians on TV that it is only *more* violence that puts an end to *some* violence. As the reality of actual American soldiers on Arab soil settled upon our school, a giddy murmur traveled up the sixth-grade rows: Would the Americans be as good-looking as the ones on TV?

Given the news of impending good-looking Americans in our city, I could barely focus on school all day! In math class I scribbled a poem, the words bursting forth from me like a geyser, which reminds me that Mrs. Adila spent a chunk of the class lecturing us that it's actually the oil gushers, and not world peace, that the American military are here for. (A wet blanket, that one.)

Anyhoo—if you can believe it, Allah—writing the poem only took me two minutes. I'm sure even the famous poets take much longer than that! It is called "The Gold," but it isn't really about gold. I'm not sure what it's about, but it's very deep.

> **The Gold by Mona Hasan, 11¼**
> Behold!
> The yellow bendable metal glimmers
> And shimmers
> But sometimes all that glitters is not gold
> It could be shiny mold
> Be wise, like a person old
> And question everything you are ~~sold~~ told.

At home this evening, Aba found out about the jammed cassette player. I told a lie. I said that I saw Tutoo stuff my bracelet charm into it on purpose because she hates listening to his tape with the song "Ebony and Ivory" over and over again. Aba's face fell. Stevie Wonder is his favorite musician.

Sunday, January 20, 1991

Ami let us watch a horror movie last night. It was so scary that now Tutoo has to keep guard outside the washroom whenever I go! It's the sort of movie that only grown-ups and older kids should watch, but Ami said that there's so much bad drama in the world, we might as well watch the made-up monsters on TV to take our minds off the real ones.

I went down to Laila's after school today. Her four-bedroom, two-balcony apartment is the exact same as ours except that hers is on the northwest corner and ours sits three floors higher, on the southeast corner. We thumbed through her new beauty magazines that her aunt had bought her from Beirut. The magazines had pictures of beautiful Lebanese women and pictures of the skin-lightening lotions and potions that can turn you into a beautiful woman. Our mothers are into such lotions and potions, but Laila and I don't see the point. Why would we want to look like anyone else?

Laila's aunt hid the magazines under a bunch of underwear in her suitcase so that the censor-wallahs wouldn't take a black marker to all the exposed haram skin. We flipped through the pictures of women wearing short, sparkly dresses. They were standing with their arms above their heads or crossed behind their backs. Were they "captives" too? They seemed trapped on the page, but something in their eyes glowed with a kind of bravery. Or maybe the word I'm thinking of is *defiance*—d-e-f-i-a-n-c-e? Or maybe I'm 100 percent wrong and it was defeat.

Anyway, much more importantly for me, I noticed that all the women had breasts as big as bowling balls!! I've already had a few PT classes full of sports but am still flat as a chapati. I'm being patient but do hurry, Allah!

Monday, January 21, 1991

Uncle Annoying dropped by today. This time he didn't even try to tickle me. He went straight to Tutoo and picked her up from behind. She fought and kicked, but being only eight and skinny like a twig, she was no match for him, and they ended up on the sofa with her squirming on his lap. My little sister is MY little sister. The only person to annoy and bother her should be *me*, so I marched over and pinched Uncle Annoying on the arm, grabbing the skin between my fingernails and squeezing until my knuckles turned white. He yelped and let go. "Oh my, you're spicy, aren't you?" he said with watery eyes, then he sheepishly released Tutoo and spent the remainder of his time rubbing his arm.

Helping my sister escape creepy Uncle Annoying might mean that I'm turning into a feminist. Laila did warn me that a book-reading mother *is* a gateway into many of the haram *isms*, like feminism and skepticism, and according to Aba, Ami *is* a voracious reader. Could it be?

Tuesday, January 22, 1991

I wrote to Otto, the cartoon mascot of *Young Times*, which is "the ultimate children's magazine in the Middle Eastern Gulf," asking him how to know if I'm a feminist. I also attached my masterpiece, "The Gold," since they are always on the lookout for "young talent" because . . . well, is there even such a thing as "old talent"?

> Dear Otto,
>
> My name is Mona Hasan. Otto, you are not only the cartoon mascot of *Young Times*, but you are also a good alien from outer space. You know everything! Can you please explain to me what a feminist is and how would I tell if I am one? Enclosure: an original poem for publication, "The Gold."

Later in the evening, I went to a movie rental store with Aba and Tutoo. Like I mentioned, my plan is to watch movies with women characters and see what I really think about being a feminist. I browsed the movie titles and posters for a very long time, and I think I finally found something that could be feminist. It's called *Aliens*, and it's about a woman astronaut who fights bad aliens. I could tell the video store clerk was impressed by my choice. Perhaps he is a budding feminist like me. He stared at my chest the whole time, so perhaps that is *budding* too. About time!

Wednesday, January 23, 1991

Tutoo and I watched *Aliens* after school but it was another Very Scary Movie. I might need washroom guarding until the end of the year! In the movie, the woman astronaut's name was Ripley. She had short hair and didn't wear any lipstick. She sweated a lot too. From her *face*! Definitely going off feminism.

In unrelated news, today's sport was badminton. Now here's a sport I could play for hours! No heavy rackets, no hard balls. It felt like ballet on the gym floor as that fluffy, white shuttlecock bounced gracefully back and forth over the net. Mrs. Naz kept saying "shuttlecock" and snickering and nudging Mrs. Adila with her elbows. What's so funny about the elegant shuttlecock, Allah? Grown-ups can be so strange sometimes.

On the way back from the gym, we ran into the eighth-grade boys returning from a field trip. They were sweaty from their long bus ride. Some of them had unbuttoned the top parts of their dress shirts and folded their sleeves up. I could see beads of sweat glistening in the hollows of their necks. One of the boys—a tall, pudgy one—walked by super slowly, chewing gum and staring at me.

Thursday, January 24, 1991

It took three phone calls and over two hours, but I asked Laila who asked Sobia who asked her older brother who asked his best friend who asked his cousin, and we finally found out that the slow-walking gum-chomper's name is Waleed. What I remember most about Waleed is that he had curly hair. A mole on the left cheek, a dimple on the right. Two of his top buttons were unbuttoned. His dress shirt wasn't properly tucked in, and his shoelaces weren't neatly tied either. Silly boy, he could trip!

Meanwhile, Ami and Aba went to a work party at Aba's bank. All the offices are throwing fancy work parties right now so people can take their minds off the Iraq-Kuwait situation. Neighbor Auntie (our next-door neighbor whose husband died young, and she never remarried because she refused to do something called "settling") came over to put us to bed tonight. It's possible that she knows a thing or two about feminism and I almost asked her but then I came to my senses! It's unlikely she does know anything at all, being that she's ancient and frumpy.

Friday, January 25, 1991

Aba and Ami came home late from their work party. They spent the morning and most of the afternoon sleeping with their bedroom door locked. When our parents finally emerged from the bedroom, they were still in pajamas, humming to themselves. They looked like they hadn't slept a wink! I guess all that worrying about Iraqi chemicals has tired them out.

Saturday, January 26, 1991

TERRIBLE BREAKING NEWS!

At lunchtime, Laila reported that her nanny, Maria-Helena dos Santos Fernandes, is leaving!! She's decided to move back to the Philippines because of the war and everyone's panic. This is very sad and upsetting for Laila and me because firstly, Maria-Helena has been Laila's nanny since the first grade, and secondly, where will we get our pansit, or yummy homemade noodles, now?!!! Laila's mother told Laila that her nineteen-year-old cousin from Cairo is coming to stay with them until May and will watch Laila for a few months, after which Laila will have to learn how to take care of herself!!

Laila's older cousin's name is Hala, and Laila told me that "Hala is coming from Cairo to stay with us because she's been 'bad.' Do you know what this means for us, Mona? A) She knows all about life, capital *L*; and B) We're going to learn all kinds of new stuff."

Laila asked what's the baddest thing I've done. I told her about pinching Uncle Annoying on the arm. She told me he sounds terrible and said that last week, when her mother took her bra shopping at the mall, some dirty old man pinched Laila's butt. Laila told her mother, who turned around and swore at the man in Arabic, and a little circle of angry women formed around him but the dirty old man pretended to be blind, so some younger men helped the dirty old man out of the mall and across the parking lot and into his car.

In the evening, I went to say goodbye to Laila's nanny and saw that everything Maria-Helena owns was laid out on her small bedroom floor. After Laila's mom scanned through it to make sure Maria-Helena was not stealing her Beautiful Woman lotions or potions, Laila and I helped Maria-Helena pack. We scooped and folded and squished almost four years of her life into one small blue suitcase. Then we watched Maria-Helena vacuum her room and strip her bed of her favorite floral bedsheets and do the laundry. We saw her start to weep when she went to hang the laundry, but still Laila and I didn't ask for her new mailing address. We also didn't hold her by the ankles and howl for her to stay. We knew our parents would get very mad if we did any of those things. Instead we made a mixtape of all of Maria-Helena's favorite songs, put heart stickers on the cassette tape box, hid it when we arrived, and then tucked it into her thin blue suitcase as a surprise. Then we let Maria-Helena go quietly, as if the goodbye didn't break our hearts in two.

Sunday, January 27, 1991

Ami hates when we do this, but we ate dinner in front of the TV. Most of Dubai did the same thing tonight. America dropped more bombs on Iraq yesterday. Because of this,

Iraq's president blew up Kuwait's oil wells because . . . well, because *RETALIATION*, of course. The TV screen flickered with yellow and red flames, and plumes of black smoke rose millions of feet high. I think the black smoke set against the desert sand might make for an interesting painting, and I'll give it a go tomorrow in art class.

I flipped through my big book *Classic Paintings by the Masters* and saw that a great artist named Pablo Picasso also made a painting when a war happened close by to where he lived. He called his painting *Guernica*. I shall title mine *Baghdad Burning but They Are Watching the Oil Fields*. Hopefully my painting shall make me filthy rich one day too!

After we watched the news, Aba switched the TV off and told us to get ready for the beach. At the beach, the sky moved in swirls of pink and orange as the sun dipped into the sea. How could the sky look so peaceful in one place and be so frightful in another? We saw a plane make an arc across the pastel sky. It twinkled as it went by. Maybe this was Maria-Helena's plane taking her away toward her brand-new life, so Tutoo and I waved, just in case.

Tutoo and I know our parents are worried about the war and so even though we had plenty of questions about it, we didn't bring it up to them and let them enjoy the sounds of the sea instead.

My questions and emotions bubbled on the inside, so out gushed another poem that I jotted down hastily at the beach—

The Sea by Mona Hasan, 11¼
Woe is me
Sitting by the sea
Under a palm tree
Thinking how can it be?
Why does the world fail to see
All the pain around me.

I still haven't heard back from Otto, the mascot of *Young Times*, "the ultimate children's magazine in the Middle Eastern Gulf." Perhaps he is confused by feminism too. But it is odd that he hasn't been in touch to discuss publishing my original poetic masterpiece, "The Gold." My brilliance can be too much sometimes.

Monday, January 28, 1991

Today's washroom stall read "SLUTTING IS HARAM" and there were fiery squiggles around the words. I suppose the squiggles were meant to be the flames of hell, like the ones from the Kuwaiti oil wells yesterday. I hope the mystery artist eventually spells this word correctly. It's so confusing! *SLUT* is both something you can *be* and something you can *do*?!

In other news, Aba came home early with a cardboard box filled with masking tape. The word at his office and in the shisha cafés is that Iraq's president has been using chemicals to kill people and likely we're next. Aba's already lived through the Pakistan-Bangladesh war of 1971, and before that his parents lived through the Partition of India in 1947 when the country cleaved into two (a new India and Pakistan), so Aba's not too worried about dying. He is worried about *how* he dies though. He'd prefer bombs, not chemicals. All the stores have run out of gas masks, so Aba was left to buy a box of masking tape to seal our window frames. All this time, I had thought wars happened in far-off places to far-off people, and now I know that the truth is that they can happen to anyone! Anywhere. Anytime.

Aba positioned long strips of masking tape against all the window frames in our apartment. Tutoo and I flattened the air bubbles using our palms. Ami chain-smoked in the kitchen. Since the cassette player is still broken, we turned the radio up and sang along off-key to *Top of the Pops*. Later Tutoo and I took the radio into her room and disco-danced and belly-danced until we ended up on the floor crying because we were laughing so much.

Before bedtime, more verses came bubbling to the surface, and Tutoo agreed that these were my best ones yet!

The Ebb and the Flow by Mona Hasan, 11¼
Iraqi gas may come and life may go
So let's bury the panic and disco
This is life's ebb and flow

Tuesday, January 29, 1991

Good news—I finally received a letter from Otto today! Bad news—I can't make heads or tails of it!

Dear Mona,

Thank you for your letter. It was passed around our office and provoked much discussion.

Simply put, a feminist questions the world she sees and dreams of a better one. We encourage you to continue to pay attention to the world around you, after which we advise a prolonged period of quiet reflection. Deep in the depths of your gut, question if alternative worlds are desirable or possible.

Whilst your poem "The Gold" shows promise, our editorial panel has regrettably deemed it of not sufficient quality for publication at this time. That being so, you should know that we encourage you to continue down the path of a poet, howsoever laden with rejection and hardship it may be. This world (and any imagined better one) certainly needs more poets.

Best,

Otto

Your friendly neighborhood alien from a distant galaxy and now a cartoon mascot for *Young Times,* "the ultimate children's magazine in the Middle Eastern Gulf."

Having read between the lines, isn't it grand, Allah, that Otto himself has told me that I possess the natural talent and superior intelligence to pursue a full-time career as a Poetess?!

Wednesday, January 30, 1991

Gym Day today and we tried another sport I've never tried before—"volleyball."

We split into teams of six this time. We threw the hard white ball over the net using our palms, wrists and forearms. Mrs. Naz read off the types of throws we could make from a long piece of paper: "digs," "sets" and "spikes."

I know the new principal wants us to feel like we are equal to the boys—wants us to believe that we can do anything boys can do—but by the end of class, our wrists and arms were bruised and some of us had even broken fingernails. There were a lot of tears. Now we know for sure that we are *NOT* equal to the boys! We are far weaker and should be allowed to stay that way! Mr. Qadri is a feminist! We hate him.

In the middle of a volley, I glanced over and there was Waleed by the gym doors, looking in with a big grin. We locked eyes. I felt my heart jump. The ground beneath me shifted. It may have been because the white volleyball came flying toward me and knocked me on my head. Hard. I fell. From my horizontal vantage point on the gym floor, I saw that Waleed's shoelaces were untied. *Again!* What a mess he is! Who would help him if he tripped? And what if he scraped his knee? I suppose I would have to use the hem of my skirt to dab at the wound gently . . .

Thursday, January 31, 1991

Oh, Allah, why do we use words? They are the most confusing tool we have.

What we tell each other with our eyes is crystal clear.

CHAPTER TWO

February

Friday, February 1, 1991

Went over to Laila's today to meet her older babysitting cousin, Hala.

She was a tornado of chocolate skin and curly hair. She whirled into Laila's bedroom and cornered me right away:

"You're Laila's little friend. The brain."

"Um, yes."

"What are they teaching you over at that girls' prison?"

"Uh . . . we just started fractional integrals in math and, uh, in science, we're studying osmosis and the rain cycle and, uh . . ."

"What do you know about the Prophet's wives?"

"You mean the wives of our esteemed messenger of Allah, the Venerable Hazrat Muhammad (peace be upon him)?"

"Yeah, him."

"Uh, well, uh . . . I know he had four wives. The esteemed Hazrat Khadijah (peace be upon her) was the first and the esteemed Hazrat Ayesha (peace be upon her), uh, was the last and . . ."

"Ha! The same vomit. Khadijah was forty and Ayesha was nine when he married them. They talk to you girls about that yet?"

I *did* know that the Prophet married Khadijah when *he* was twenty-five and *she* was forty, but I never really thought about it. At forty, Khadijah must've been wrinkly, white-haired and . . . and . . . decrepit! Maybe she didn't even have teeth. *Disgusting!*

But definitely not as disgusting as marrying a nine-year-old. No teacher has ever mentioned that. Is Hala telling the truth, Allah?

I didn't get to ask her what *SLUT* means either. I'll have to visit again to find out.

Saturday, February 2, 1991

CAPITAL *H* HORROR!

Yesterday's issue of *Young Times* had a black-and-white photo of the perfect new girl, Maryam, on page three. *Young Times* had published her poem. She was beaming up at me from the magazine, looking radiant. Her poem was a fourteen-line ~~sonnet~~ hokum entitled "Unity," and it was about regional harmony after the Gulf War.

Everyone at school crowded around her this morning, and she has become very popular. Many of our classmates have taken to walking with her arm-in-arm during lunch and recess.

Personally I think the world has gone mad, and I'm not sure how much more I can take.

Sunday, February 3, 1991

Mayday! Mayday! Ami in mad-mom mode.

"Pick up after yourselves! Clean your filthy rooms!" she grumbled as soon as Tutoo and I were back from school.

What my mother doesn't know is that if my belongings are neatly tucked away in drawers and closets, I completely forget I have them. I've decided to head over to Laila's instead.

Monday, February 4, 1991

Laila and I begged Hala to tell us what *SLUT* means but she wouldn't explain it. Hala is our only ticket to understanding Mystery Words, so we pleaded for a long time. She dismissed us, saying that to fully understand some words, you have to climb a mountain of other words and that Laila and I have only just learned to walk, let alone climb! She dead would not budge! "The truth is, I'm still learning about that word myself," she said, shrugging, so we gave up. Then she flicked her hair and asked if we knew anything about tongue-kissing.

"Oh, yes. Everything, of course," Laila answered and I bobbled my head next to her in agreement. Hala narrowed her eyes at us and explained it anyway.

Y   U   C   K   !   !   !

Ya Allah, it's the grossest thing I've ever heard!! I don't even know if I believe it!! It's just too ridiculous to be true! When two people move their lips closer together on TV, the screen always cuts to a picture of a mosque or a field of flowers! Hala said that if everyone knew about tongue-kissing, then everyone would start doing it and no one would be able to stop doing it, and if no one would be able to stop doing it, then everyone would stop eating and *DIE*! It feels that good, Hala said.

That good touching someone's slimy snot-stopper with your own squishy, mushy mucus-magnet?!

Disgusting!!!

Right, Allah?

Tuesday, February 5, 1991

At dinnertime Ami complained to Aba about my messy room: "If this girl doesn't learn how to keep a clean house, then I'm afraid no one will marry her." My mother is always afraid that no one will want to marry me. Ami tried to brush her fears onto Aba about families being scared to marry their sons off to an untidy girl like me. But ya Allah, I am so lucky—my father stuck up for me!

"Enough with this nonsense!" Aba told Ami. He reminded her that a Dubai banker's daughter would always be considered a good catch and that they have nothing to worry about. He assured her that both Tutoo and I would be out of their hair soon enough, then they both laughed heartily and went to bed early.

I guess that's that, then! I will be married when I'm twenty-two and I will finally escape my mother's control. After that, it will only be my husband who tells me what to do.

Wednesday, February 6, 1991

During PT class, Waleed sauntered by the open gym doors with two other boys. One of his friends threw me a peace sign and shot me a goofy grin. But my eyes were on Waleed and his eyes were on me. No grin, no smile this time. Just unmoving, unblinking staring with those dark, wet eyes of his. It felt like I was caught in a thunderstorm.

No wonder we are supposed to lower our gaze! This staring-into-the-eyes is risky business, isn't it?

I'm not sure how exchanging spit could ever feel better than *this*.

Thursday, February 7, 1991

Tongue-kissing must be terrible to watch! That's why they don't show it on TV. It must look like two people vomiting into each other's mouths. Grown-ups are *SO* disgusting! It's just so awful that I can't stop thinking about it!

Friday, February 8, 1991

Underneath her party saris, Ami keeps a small tower of naughty books. *The Fountain of Love. An Eternal Flame. The Lady and the Lace. A Gentleman's Promise.*

I'm starting with *A Gentleman's Promise*. There is sure to be lots in here about tongue-kissing. I just need to know a few extra details. To know exactly what I should avoid, of course.

> **A Kiss by Mona Hasan, 11¼**
> Whatever is a tongue-kiss?
> Surely something is amiss
>
> If the news shows us missiles and guts
> But the TV always cuts
>
> Two lips coming closer for a tongue-kiss . . .
> Is it a disgusting thing or is it total bliss?

Saturday, February 9, 1991

Valentine's Day is coming up! It's kind of a big deal in Dubai, mostly because it's not supposed to be a big deal in Dubai.

If Waleed has the L-feelings for me, then that's the day he should declare them! If he's a real boy, anyway. I know it's not very "fair" or "feminist" of me to pile the pressure on him but let's face it: No proper girl can declare her L-feelings *first* and especially *not* on Valentine's Day. It's just not very *seemly*, is it?

I spent the day sculpting and painting papier-mâché hearts for the same people I do every year—my parents, Tutoo and Laila. But I did make two extra hearts for Hala and Neighbor Auntie this year, since I felt poorly for them. Being unmarried at their ages, it must be terribly lonesome. Whatever do they do with all their free time not cooking and cleaning for others? Attending to their own desires, I suppose. Sounds like a pretty ~~ideal~~ sad situation.

Monday, February 11, 1991

When Tutoo and I came home from school, we found Ami in her bedroom under the covers.

She complained that not having a driving license was tiring, demeaning and *wah, wah, wah*. She refused to get up, and Tutoo and I had to make our own dinner. We assembled pita wraps with cold tandoori chicken and store-bought tabbouleh. We added a dollop of mango chutney and a spread of hummus. We ate our Desi-Arab mishmash in front of the TV, and when Aba came home from work, he did the same.

Before bedtime, I went to see Ami and ask her what was truly wrong. "Ennui," she said and sighed.

I looked up *ennui* in the dictionary, but I haven't a clue how domestic monotony would make my mother too tired to carry out her maternal duties and fix us our dinner. I kept quiet though. Alas, my father did not reprimand her either. It appears that *both* my parents are feeble, and I must have the strength to bear it.

Tuesday, February 12, 1991

It'd been a while since we'd seen Uncle Annoying but he came over tonight. I set up the chessboard so there would be no more tickle games. He wanted to play his first match against Tutoo and promised me one another time. I stuck around and studied their game closely.

I watched him lose—*on purpose!*

He deliberately ignored three chances to take Tutoo's queen. Then he let Tutoo corner him in checkmate. He clapped his hands in mock surprise, then went on and on about how smart and special Tutoo is: "Can you believe it? Tutoo beat *ME!* She's the smartest and most special girl in all of Dubai, isn't she?" Tutoo grinned from ear to ear and beamed with pride. I felt my stomach lurch. Before he left, I saw him sneak a fistful of candy to Tutoo. She refused to share! Felt uneasy. Went to bed.

I tossed and turned most of the night.

Woke up in the middle of the night ~~thinking~~ knowing that at his next visit, I need to do something about Uncle Annoying's annoyingness.

But what?

Scribbled this note in my journal and went back to bed.

Wednesday, February 13, 1991

Waleed passed by the gymnasium at 11:42 a.m. I was in the hallway getting a drink from the water fountain and leaving a special gift for a special someone. When Waleed walked by, Laila nudged me in the ribs and I straightened up just in time to give him a ~~bug-eyed glare~~ sultry stare. He walked straight into a pillar and hit his head.

Mrs. Naz choose that same instant to yell at Laila and me to get back inside the gymnasium. On the way in, I discreetly pointed to the water fountain.

Waleed understood and casually made his way over, and that's when I saw the sun and the stars! His face lit up and he looked back at me with the biggest boy-smile I've ever seen! He picked up the little red heart that I'd left for him. The heart was hand-painted with the letters "wow" for Waleed and "meem" for Mona. He slipped my homemade heart into his front pocket.

His smile told me everything I needed to know. This is it—the big *L*!

And here I had believed that Love was something that happened in far-off places to far-off people! I guess the truth is that it can happen to anyone. Anywhere. Anytime.

Thursday, February 14, 1991

Today the intercom trilled at first period, and Mr. Qadri's voice came over the speaker: "Ladies and, uh ... little ladies. Attention. Attention. Attention, please. I have a special announcement to make. In November 1989, the Berlin Wall fell. East and West tore down the wall separating them. This historical event reminds us that we have more that connects us than what divides us. In honor of that momentous moment, today the divisions between the boys' and girls' sections will come down for thirty minutes during lunchtime. Yes, today under the vigilant and hovering supervision of your teachers, the boys' section and the girls' section will have combined lunchtime in the courtyard! This is [*cough*] *NOT* [*cough*] in celebration of Valentine's Day. I repeat, this is *NOT* in any way to honor the dishonorable Valentine's Day; rather, this co-mingling is to inspire a history lesson on the Berlin Wall ... [*cough*]. Attention over." There was stunned silence. Then nervous clapping. Had Mr. Qadri lost his mind? Suffered heat stroke, maybe?

At lunchtime, Laila and I sat on the stairs by the girls' building, delicately nibbling our lunches. The boys came stampeding out of the boys' building and roamed the girls' field.

Waleed strode up to me confidently. Handsomely. When he was but a few steps from my feet, he bowed with a flourish. Cleared his throat. He clutched his chest with his left palm and extended his open right palm toward me. He began—

> Behold, ye peasants!
> My eyes feast upon the most beauteous beauty
> > I ever did see!
> On bended knee,
> Mona Hasan of Dubai, I declare that my heart
> > belongs to thee!

Then Mrs. Naz rapped the wooden ruler on my desk. "Mona! Mona!! Earth to Mona!!!"

My daydream shattered.

What really happened at lunchtime was that the boys moped in one half of the field, heads down, and the girls moped in the other. From across the space, Waleed and I eyed each other like ~~stealthy lion and graceful gazelle~~ nervous wet mice, and before we knew it, the bell rang and lunchtime was over.

Friday, February 15, 1991

Waleed. Waleed.

Waleed. Waleed. Waleed. Waleed. Waleed. Waleed. Waleed.
Waleed. Waleed. Waleed. Waleed. Waleed. Waleed. Waleed.
Waleed. Waleed. Waleed. Waleed. Waleed. Waleed. Waleed.
Waleed. Waleed. Waleed. Waleed. Waleed. Waleed. Waleed.
Waleed. Waleed. Waleed. Waleed. Waleed. Waleed. Waleed.
Waleed. Waleed. Waleed. Waleed. Waleed. Waleed. Waleed.
Waleed. Waleed. Waleed. Waleed. Waleed. Waleed. Waleed.
Waleed. Waleed. Waleed. Waleed.

Monday, February 18, 1991

Aba fumed about the broken cassette player all evening. He
has not been able to listen to "Ebony and Ivory" for a month
and a half now, and we're not sure how he's lasted this long.
He wanted to punish Tutoo by taking away her Atari joystick for two weeks, but I advised Tutoo to LDD and he
threw his hands in the air and returned the joystick, and
Tutoo and I enjoyed a game of Pac-Man instead.

LDD, or Lying Down Dead, is an old trick Tutoo and I
have been using against our parents since forever. We're
not sure how or when we came up with this genius idea. All
we know is that it works each and every time—we starfish on
the floor, belly up, and squeeze our eyes tightly shut. We make
sure not to open our eyes or move or giggle or respond in
any way. The parents then have no choice but to give in to our
demands! We do make sure not to use it *too* often though,
but tonight counted as a Critical and Necessary Situation

45

(CNS) and I allowed Tutoo to use LDD. However, she is now banned from using it for the next three months.

Two more sleeps before gym class.

Tuesday, February 19, 1991

ONE MORE SLEEP!!!!!

Wednesday, February 20, 1991

CAPITAL *W* WOE.

Mrs. Naz kept the gym doors locked during today's gym class. The agony I was in during the whole class! When she opened the doors for our walk back to the girls' side, the hallway was empty.

> **The Empty Hallway by Mona Hasan, 11¼**
> The empty hallway
> Caused a sad day.
>
> Now upon my bed I lay
> And wonder what may
> Never come my way.
>
> Oh, what a sad day
> Because of an empty hallway.

Sunday, February 24, 1991

Today's entry might be my most important one yet!

The Gulf War's "ground offensive" launched today! The TV people said that American soldiers went into Kuwait to fight Iraqi soldiers in hand-to-hand combat. *Finally!* The much-promised "boots on the ground"! The "ground offensive" is the TRUE start of the Gulf War, isn't it? Now with boots-on-ground and eyeball-to-eyeball fighting, it won't feel like a video game anymore, will it, Allah?

Iraq's president has promised the "mother of all battles," so this is going to be a long, lethal, bloody war. The newspeople recited over and over that Iraq's president and the Iraqi army are STUBBORN, PROUD and VENGEFUL— that's in the Arab blood, they said. This war will not end quickly *or* easily! This war will still be happening when I have *my* children, my *grandchildren* and my *great-grandchildren*!

I will record everything that happens during this lengthy and protracted war. As usual the grown-ups will be too busy to appreciate History as it unfolds, and it will fall upon us sensitive young adults to make sense of it all.

Monday, February 25, 1991

Second proper day of the ground offensive! Decided to pen the opening stanza of what is sure to become my magnus opus, "The Gulf War"—

The Gulf War by Mona Hasan, 11¼
The Gulf War will last for many ages
The Coalition will save the Kuwaitis trapped
   in their golden cages
The Gulf War will be written about in millions
   of pages
The Gulf War will last for many ages!

Tuesday, February 26, 1991

Third proper day of the *real* GULF WAR!

Not a good-looking soldier or warplane in sight! Tutoo and I spent the evening in our best party dresses *just in case.* As an afterthought, we strapped our skateboarding helmets on too. *Again: just in case.*

Wednesday, February 27, 1991

The ground-offensive part of the Gulf War is *OVER!*

We didn't even get any days off school!

Just my luck.

In the end, there was no *ground* offensive as the Americans had promised. Instead the Americans did an aerial—a-e-r-i-a-l—offensive on a highway in Iraq. The six-lane highway is now being called the Highway of Death. The mood on English TV was celebratory, but the mood on Arab TV was dead somber.

Ami said she was expecting the end of the war to feel jubilant, not gruesome. I know what she means. I was expecting to see a sheet of doves in the sky. Tutoo said she was expecting new schools and roads and hospitals to replace the ones that the Americans had bombed. I still think doves would've done the trick.

We went out for dinner to mark the end of the Gulf War, but Tutoo had to be dragged along. She didn't want to celebrate. She complained that the bloodshed had ruined her appetite! I reminded her that "only three hundred eighty-three Americans died, Tutoo. That's not very bloody for a war." I was proud of myself for having memorized the number from TV. But Tutoo responded with, "Yes, but how many Iraqis, Mona?" I dismissed her with the back of my hand. "Don't be ridiculous, Tutoo. No one on TV keeps a count of dead Iraqi bodies."

At the restaurant, Tutoo barely touched her charcoal-grilled lamb kebabs, so I ate her share. *YUM!*

On the car ride home, the sky was pitch-black and a luminous moon followed us the whole way. Before bedtime, Ami let us peel the masking tape off the windows. Except for a few chips and cracks, everything's back to normal, isn't it?

Thursday, February 28, 1991

The MOST urgent and pressing conundrum of 1991 is *WHEN* and *HOW* will I be able to see Waleed again??? The gym doors were closed *AGAIN* during PT class!!!!

The Closed Door by Mona Hasan, 11¼

The closed door
Is such an eyesore
It breaks my heart into four

The closed door
Is a bore, a chore and a snore
And causes anger galore!

How will it open, this door?
Because I want more.

CHAPTER THREE

March

Friday, March 1, 1991

Woke up BLEARY-EYED and EXHAUSTED this morning! There was a lot of arguing between Ami and Aba late last night. They were arguing about something called "immi-gray-shun," which I will have to look up later. Whatever it is, they both agreed that it needed to happen, but they disagreed on the timing. Ami insisted that "now" was the best time for it. She spoke to Aba like he was a little child and said that there had been no "regime change" and that mayhem was still around the corner. Aba said that one must always look at the world with rose-colored glasses, and Ami snapped that one should never forget that roses came with thorns.

They argued back and forth until Ami got the last line in—"If money can't buy us peace when we need it, then what's the point?" There was silence after that. Whatever did she mean? Not enough money to buy peace?? But isn't the Gulf War over?!

The end result of all the bickering was that Aba slept in his study, which is next to my bedroom. His snoring kept me up all night! I do wish my parents would be a bit more thoughtful. Here I am going through the pangs of love and I desperately need my beauty sleep. I suppose I can't expect my parents to know what love and sacrifice are all about. They have been married for twelve and a half years, after all.

Saturday, March 2, 1991

Last I saw Waleed was on Valentine's Day—more than TWO WEEKS AGO!!!

How can I be expected to carry on like this if we never see each other again?! Only loneliness and suffering stretch ahead of me. The silver lining is that I now understand heartache like all the greatest poets of yore. My suffering will serve as a boon to my balladry, won't it, Allah?

Heartache by Mona Hasan, 11¼
My heart, it aches and breaks and I quake and
    shake
Nothing, ever, will make my pain go away—
    except maybe slices of cake.

Sunday, March 3, 1991

I begged Ami to take us to Al Ghurair mall so I could throw coins into the water fountain with the lights. I have seen kids on TV make their demands from You this same way, and after a morning of moping, pouting and loud sighing, Ami finally caved and off into a taxi we went. When we got to the right spot, I closed my eyes, tossed in three of my lucky silver dirhams and wished to see Waleed again. When we got home, I performed both my Asr and Maghrib prayers. During my duas, I bargained that I would feed the poor and hideous if You would arrange a meeting with Waleed. Later, I swiped three mangoes from our fruit bowl and stashed them in my backpack. In the morning I will give them to one of my Hindu classmates and ask her to give them to one of her Hindu gods as an offering on my behalf. I'm still figuring out which one of these pathways is the shortest one to You. It's in my best interests to experiment with and exploit each one, right, Allah?

Monday, March 4, 1991

Last week Hala told us that she is going to take all the money she makes selling her hard-to-find books and buy lipstick, nail polish and hairspray. She said she's not waiting for her parents to tell her what kind of life they've decided she should live.

"No matter the cost, you have to reach out and grab the life you want," she said. Then she went off to the Sheraton Beach Club to flirt with the British expats.

Tuesday, March 5, 1991

Went over after school to ask Hala how does one reach out and grab the life they want? I mean, I can't just open a locked gym door all by myself! I don't know any magic!

Hala told me that most of the answers to life's mysteries can be found inside books. She said that the time had come for me to read what are considered the classics. She then lent me a four-hundred-page beast of a book titled *Jane Eyre* by authoress Charlotte Brontë. I'm really hoping this book is full of helpful advice on how to get an eighth-grade boy to fall madly in love with a sixth-grade girl, and the tips and tricks they can use to meet up!

Wednesday, March 6, 1991

No such luck. Hala informed me that the Jane in *Jane Eyre* also went to an all-girls school! I've returned the book unread—I'm afraid I can't be bothered to read it. What could this Jane possibly teach me about life, having lived such a provincial, sheltered one of her own? How could she possibly know anything useful about boys or tongue-kissing?

Hala knows all about life, capital *L*, so I asked *her* about the types of books she reads, and she told me that she likes stories from faraway places about faraway people during faraway times. Stories by Russian storytellers about life in far-off Russia during a time long ago. Authors with grand foreign names like Aleksandr Solzhenitsyn, Fyodor Dostoevsky, Lev Nikolayevich Tolstoy and Anton Chekhov.

She said that they wrote stories that could've gotten them in big trouble. About struggle and dignity, war and freedom and the human spirit prevailing under extreme conditions. Stories that were true without ever having happened.

What nonsense! How can anything be true if it's never happened?

Thursday, March 7, 1991

Gym day tomorrow. Will the gym doors be open or closed?

Open or closed?

Open or closed?

Open or closed?

Open or closed?

Friday, March 8, 1991

CLOSED!!!

!!!

Ya Allah, it seems that prayer alone is not getting me the life I want. Now what? No option but to raise the white flag and forget about seeing Waleed again, I suppose. Misery. And woe.

Thursday, March 14, 1991

Hala always says to reach out and grab the life that you want, so when no one was looking, Laila and I grabbed Mrs. Naz's can of Fanta and poured it into the air conditioner's control box. There were a few sputtering sparks and pops, and eventually the humming stopped. In thirty minutes the place was muggy and humid. Mrs. Naz finally threw open the gym doors.

Sure enough, Waleed and some of his friends walked by the gym. But as soon as they looked in, they burst out laughing. As they headed down the hallway with their loud laughter, Laila and I rushed in the other direction to the washroom. Staring back at us from the washroom mirrors was stringy hair matted on heads, large sweat stains under arms and beads of sweat on upper lips! We looked mortifyingly human! Their laughter rang in my ears all day.

Half hour before bedtime. If Waleed doesn't like me at my worst, then he's not going to get me at my best! (I found this quote in one of Laila's beauty magazines. It's by some American actress called Marilyn Monroe. I'm stealing it for myself.)

Five minutes later. Oh, Waleed, my worst is very rare!! Come back!!!! Forgive my imperfections! Love and accept me again.

Friday, March 15, 1991

Ami noticed me looking morose after school last night, so she took me bra shopping this morning to cheer me up. We went to the back of the shop, where all the haram unmentionables like Buddha statues, Sade cassettes and women's undies were shrouded. Tutoo picked out the most scandalous ones—scratchy ones in lace, confusing ones with complicated hooks, and salacious ones with hearts and lipstick marks on them! She brought them toward me and held each one up to my chest, taunting, "Jiggle, jiggle, squiggle, squiggle!"

"Amiiiiiiiiiiiiii! Tutoo's bothering me!!" I wailed.

Ami sounded off on Tutoo: "Ya Khuda! Put those haram things down this instant!!" Tutoo slunk away and re-shrouded the bras.

Ami and I argued for a few minutes about which one to buy. In fact, looking around, I could see quite a few other girls my age having arguments about their fashion choices with their mothers too.

In the end, I agreed to Ami's suggestion of a plain-white cotton bra with thick, sturdy straps, as it was the only one in my size. The lady at the shop bellowed at the pimpled teen clerk to get the smallest size from the storage room in the back. "ARREY, MOHAMMED, GO! THEY'RE IN THE BACK! DOUBLE-A CUP FOR THIS CHILD!" The mortification.

Sunday, March 17, 1991

Just realized that it's the first day of Ramadan tomorrow.

Just my luck that it crept up on me so suddenly!

Now for the next twenty-eight days or so, I'll have to hide whenever I eat or drink in public. The sacrifice and discipline required of me every year boggles my mind.

Tuesday, March 19, 1991

Someone from the Tablighi Jamaat came to our front door tonight.

The Tablighi Jamaat are a brotherhood of do-gooders from the mosque across the street. They wear full beards and have strings of prayer beads looped around their wrists. Every year during Ramadan, someone from the Tablighi Jamaat knocks on our door. They try to convince my father to join them at the mosque for the special evening prayers. Every Ramadan they fail.

Since as long as I can remember, Aba avoids them. He usually eyes them in the parking lot. Then he beelines it to the elevator. Sprints from elevator to front door. Comes in through the front door huffing and puffing. Shrugs off his shoes. Loosens his necktie. Pulls off his socks and tosses them, in little balls, down the front hallway. "Tell them I'm not here," he says, jogging past me into his study, briefcase still tightly clutched.

This year the Tablighi Jamaat sent a tall ebony-colored beanpole to try to entice my father. Beanpole knocked non-stop at the door for two minutes. I opened it a crack after studying him through the peephole. To me, he looked like a new convert. I saw the telltale signs of a fresh beard—baby hairs sprouting on his chin and cheeks.

"As-salamu alaikum wa-rahmatu-llahi wa-barakatuh, little sister," he said lyrically, pausing in all the right places. Yep. New convert.

"Big brother, my mother is napping. Your knocking is going to land us in big trouble."

"Little sister, ask your father to come to the door."

"Um, uh, he's not home."

The new convert frowned. "But little sister, I saw him in the parking lot."

"Uh, um, I mean he's in the washroom?"

"Little sister, lying during Ramadan is the sin of sins. But fear not, Allah will surely forgive a girl child. But then again, why should we tempt the wrath and fury of the all-knowing, all-powerful Allah? Little sister, go. Go now. Tell your father through the washroom door that I am part of the honorable Tablighi Jamaat, and I came only to say salaam to my brother. And also I came only to tell him that Allah loves him. And last thing, tell him that it would be my humblest desire to have him join me in harmonious, night-long prayer. Another last thing, tell him that the Tablighi Jamaat are now a very *modern* group—we take credit cards for all our charitable donations . . ."

I told the New Convert that I'd pass the information on to my father. Then I closed the door and turned the lock, sliding the chain-lock noisily into place, and walked into my father's study.

Aba was already out of his work clothes, lounging in his undershirt and loose underwear, watching Jacques Cousteau on the big, boxy TV.

"Is he gone?" Aba asked.

"I think so." I shrugged. On the grainy screen, hermit crabs scuttled across large rocks on a cold, deserted island. The skinny French explorer with a red cap looked despondent. Man's greed for plastic was destroying nature.

Then we heard it. Knocking at the front door. Gentle but persistent.

Aba turned the volume up on the TV and I sat cross-legged on the floor. Seconds later, Tutoo appeared and joined me. Together, the three of us we watched Cousteau dive into the cold, silent depths of the Indian Ocean. "Il faut aller voir," said Cousteau in French as he plunged his skinny body into the unchartered ocean. Aba turned to us and said, "Girls,

Cousteau is telling us 'one must go and see,' but what he means is that one must explore to see."

Wednesday, March 20, 1991

Another thing that happens every year during Ramadan is that all the city's Muslim laborers meet in public parks to break their fasts together.

They gather in a shady part of the fields, cradling teeming pots and bowls and dishes, and spread colorful bedsheets on the grass. They arrange their dishes on the ground, and when they hear the call to prayer, they sip water, nibble on dates and rush into mosques for the first prayer. After this first, breaking-fast prayer, they pour out of the mosques and settle in for the real meal. They uncover their bowls of rice and dal and curries and rotis and fruit.

It's the one time of the year when I see all of Dubai's drivers and shopkeepers, construction workers and waiters and dishwashers and security guards, janitors and bricklayers and mechanics all in the same space at the same time. Like the rest of Dubai, I sometimes forget they are there. But Aba says this country was built, and continues to be built, from the sweat off their backs, which is news to me because their stories are nowhere! They're voiceless, I guess. Or is it that they are unheard?

Anyhoo, amongst themselves, these poor people sure eat a lot. And laugh a lot too!

I look down on them from the thirty-second floor. I wrap myself in my mother's favorite silk curtains and munch on Swiss chocolate bars, taking care not to leave any stains on the fabric.

They're so very different from me, aren't they, Allah? Their food would probably be much too spicy for me, wouldn't it? Their jokes much too different?

Thursday, March 21, 1991

Reporting from the grounds of Sheikha Khalidiya, here is the latest development from the boys' section:

TODAY I RECEIVED THE FIRST TOKEN (MANY MORE TO FOLLOW, OF COURSE) OF ETERNAL AND UNDYING LOVE FROM MY ONE TRUE LOVE!!!

Waleed gave a little piece of purple paper that he'd origami-folded into a swan to his cousin, who gave it his best friend, who passed it on to his sister, who gave it to Laila, who slipped it to me during the last class of the day! Now this tiny piece of paper—a symbol of Waleed's everlasting love for me—sits quivering in my sweaty left hand, as I write with my quivering right hand.

A SWAN!!!!

!!!!

They mate for life, don't they?

Friday, March 22, 1991

Tutoo is jealous of my swan. She's super into animals right now. I have to hide it carefully. Laila understands because she has two little brothers. They are always snooping around her things and stealing her treasures too.

It's Friday, so no school today, and we spent the morning at the beach. Later in the day, when we were home and I was washing up, I heard Tutoo rummaging through my desk drawers looking for my swan! I barged in and screamed at her for twenty minutes. What a nosy little booger she is! Bad news for her—she doesn't know that I hid the swan under my pillow!

Half hour before bedtime. My cheeks are wet from all the tears and snot that ran down them today! Tutoo found the swan under my pillow and was playing with it this evening! I came upon her from behind and jumped on her, and we fought to the death on the floor. I felt today was the day I would break her nose, her ears, her entire booger head! Aba came running in and pushed us into different corners. Ami was looking in from the doorway, yelling at us to calm down. They both looked so disgusted that we were fighting over a piece of paper. Fools! What could they possibly know about matters of the heart! I was able to get the swan back, but it's slightly ripped up and crumpled now.

Five minutes later. There was some writing inside! One unfolded wing reads—

I don't know how or why
but your eyes sparkle like a starry sky.

The other wing reads—

Sunday at 12:42 p.m. by the water fountain.

Egad! Had it not been for my pesky shrimp of a sister, I would have missed Waleed's message. I suppose there are one or two benefits to having a sibling after all.

Now to focus—Waleed has asked me to meet him in two days!!

My first date!

Saturday, March 23, 1991

A year is divided into quarters, and those quarters are very important for businesses and banks. Laila's father goes to Switzerland every quarter and brings back little bottles of sharaab, or alcohol, that the airplane woman gives him, which he then hides in his sock drawer.

Laila said her father would never notice if we took two small bottles.

She said that the sharaab will relax me for my first date! She said that the Americans and British use sharaab before all important meetings. "It's basically just medicine," she said. "Drink some. Otherwise you'll make a fool of yourself just being yourself tomorrow!" I wanted to ask Laila if drinking sharaab a full day before the date might maybe possibly cancel its potency but then I had the good sense to zip it. Laila has had a sip or two of sharaab before and is therefore far wiser than me! I took the small bottle and drank it's contents, trying my best to look grown-up and sophisticated. The beverage went down like a punch to the throat. "Delicious," I gasped.

Laila is a good friend and I will never forget the other sage advice she gave me:

1. Let the boy do all the talking;
2. Look elegant by keeping both chin and nose at a slightly high angle at all times;
3. If I must speak, use fancy American words; and lastly,
4. If he gets too fresh, kick him in the ding-dong.

I'm so nervous! *Anything* could happen tomorrow! I took one perfume-sized bottle and sipped it slowly over the hour. I didn't feel relaxed, so I took another one and gulped that one down a bit faster.

Half hour before bedtime. I have a huge headache and feel very vomit-y. It is the first time I have been drunk! Going to go lie down and have asked Tutoo to keep a cold compress on my forehead. Whatever happens, I must make it to school tomorrow!

Sunday, March 24, 1991

At 12:42 p.m., I asked for a washroom pass during PT class and went out into the empty hallway. Waleed was slumped against the wall by the water fountain. His right foot was braced against the wall with his knee casually bent. His hands were jammed into his pant pockets. His face—all eyes. My heart—pounding its way up to my throat.

"Hey."

"Um, hey."

I suddenly realized that I had a burning desire to pee. I shifted from one foot to the next and slowly began to back away. I had made it about four awkward backward steps when he blurted out:

"What's your favorite color?"

"Uh, red."

"Your favorite sport?"

"Uh, ping-pong."

"Favorite singer?"

"Uh, Tiffany."

"You don't have any brothers?"

"No."

"No older male cousins?"

"No."

"Okay, you can be my girlfriend."

"Uh, cowabunga."

"Right. But, listen, only after Ramadan is over."

"Oh."

"My parents take Ramadan very seriously. I go for Tarawih prayers every night."

"Bummer."

"So, do you want to know my favorites?"

"Uh-huh."

"Green, cricket and the Beetles."

"Gnarly."

"I'll send you another note after Ramadan is over, I guess."

"Totally tubular."

Oh, Allah, I barely managed any words! But I do think I made a good impression with the ones I did use, especially my fancy American ones that I learned from the *Teenage Mutant Ninja Turtles*! He definitely stared at me harder after I said them. My cheeks were burning, and there was so much heat inside that I was afraid I'd erupt into a fireball right then and there. I ran off to the washroom right after.

My first date was all I imagined and so much more! The only problem is that it appears it's going to take a tad longer for him to build up the courage to tongue-kiss.

Monday, March 25, 1991

Boy with the Loose Shoelace by Mona Hasan, 11¼
O! Ye boy with the loose shoelace,
Our first date was by the water fountain

It was not a mountain.
The joy in my heart upon seeing your face
Made me feel like my organs were floating in
   outer space!

Tuesday, March 26, 1991

Laila agreed with me that waiting until after Ramadan is over to see Waleed again will be the most challenging and difficult trial of my life as of yet. But we both also agreed that since all the Greats in history have suffered immensely, my time has arrived, and I can put off my Dark Night of the Soul no longer.

Thursday, March 28, 1991

MYSTERY ABOUNDS!

Ami spent an inordinate amount of time with Neighbor Auntie on the phone today. Ami kept counting days on the calendar and circling various numbers. She even tore a hole in the calendar from pressing the pen so hard on the paper. She seemed particularly worried about not being on time for some event. "I'm over three days late! I turn thirty-one this year—I thought the fertile years were over! I can't believe I'm this late." Ami gets frantic about being late in the mornings too, since if we miss the bus to school, we have to spend the day at home with her. I wonder what she's so worried about!

Saturday, March 30, 1991

Ami and Aba argued about that word *immigration* again last night—which I looked up and it appears that my parents are arguing about moving to a new country! Our parents have always blindly done whatever they've wanted, but this one would really take the cake!!

Hopefully it will all be for naught! They are, at least, in disagreement about it—my mother is in favor of leaving soon, and my father appears hesitant. During their argument tonight, my mother even swore at my father under her breath. It is a terrible thing to hear your own mother swearing. I blame it on the books she reads. Fanning the flames further, the dishes from today are still sitting in the sink, and she hasn't ironed our school uniforms either. I'm sure it will not bode well for Tutoo and me to see our mother shirking her duties thusly. I shudder at the future effects of such childhood trauma.

CHAPTER FOUR

April

Monday, April 1, 1991

My life has become difficult and taxing. How am I to shoulder such adversity? The difficult and taxing things in my life:

1. The Gulf War came and went without any days off school.
2. I have a boyfriend who only wants to talk after Ramadan is over.
3. My parents are thinking of ruining our lives by immigrating!

Things can't get much worse than this, can they?

Tuesday, April 2, 1991

Today, Mrs. Naz was carrying a stack of paper into our classroom and the stack fell just outside our classroom door. The individual sheets fanned out on the floor. The new girl, Maryam, rushed over to help and made a big show of picking them up for Mrs. Naz. In a vexing baby voice, Maryam told Mrs. Naz, "Oh, Mrs. Naz. *Allow* me to be at your *service.*"

Maryam has taken brown-nosing in our classroom to a whole new level! It is disgusting.

I had to elbow her twice in order to jump in and help with the rescue of the scattered papers. As we carefully picked them up, I looked at Maryam with cold, dark eyes. In no uncertain terms, my eyes told her: *Yalla, new girl! In this classroom, there's only enough room for one teacher's pet, and that seat's warm with my butt on it.*

Wednesday, April 3, 1991

CAPITAL *D* DRAMA!

I GOT INTO A FIGHT AT SCHOOL!

Now I know how Ripley must have felt fighting that big slimy alien at the end of *Aliens*!

It happened at lunchtime. Maryam was huddling with a gaggle of girls in a corner of the lunchroom. The group kept turning back to look at Laila and me, then bursting into giggles. After a few minutes, Maryam approached me with her crew of snickering bandits trailing behind her. I stood up, and Laila moved to the back. Hands on hips, Maryam stated smugly, "You're not going to Heaven, Mona." The group of friends who all had tights covering their whole legs looked down on me. I shrunk. I could feel my socks sliding down my knees. I stooped to pull them up.

I felt hurt and confused and my cheeks flashed red.

"Why aren't I going to Heaven?" I whined.

"Your parents married for love."

The statement hit me like a slap in the face. This was news to me. My mother snapped at my father all day. True, he took all the snapping, but could such a scandal be true? Could it be that my balding father and my cranky mother once harbored love and passion in their hearts? For *each other*, no less?! No—it could not be! I responded in the only way that made sense. I shoved Maryam's right shoulder with an open palm and pouted, "Nuh-uh! Take it back!" Maryam grabbed her shoulder and shrieked as if my hand had burned her. The girls around us gasped and fanned out. Something needed to happen next, but what exactly? Questions tumbled inside my head—how precisely does one punch someone? And where? Nose? Chin? Cheek? Would my knuckles bleed? Might I chip a nail? Would it be better to spit instead?

Still hunched over and grasping her shoulder, Maryam continued with her taunting. "Yuh-huh. *My* father said *your* father never goes to the mosque, he's *never* kept a beard *and* he reads *National Geographic*." I flinched. For as long as I could remember, Aba had indeed kept a clean-shaven face. And yes, there were stacks and stacks of yellow-bordered magazines in a corner of his home study! And okay, *my* father in a mosque? My father's favorite joke was that the only way he'd enter a mosque would be horizontally. How did she know this? And how dare she fling the truth at me so . . . so . . . publicly? She continued: "And your *mother* . . . Well, *she-e* . . ."

I didn't let her finish. There is only one thing one can do and *should* do in such a situation. I darted at Maryam. She turned to run and I yanked at her pigtail as hard as I could. Her body curved backwards. Her wrists flopped at me. She bleated like a pitiful lamb.

"Mrs. Naz! Mrs. Naz! Mrs. Naz! Oh, Mrs. Naz, do HURRY!! Mona is *killing* me!"

A side note—spitting is an art form and requires practice. My spit shot out feebly and landed on my own chin, dribbling slowly onto my blouse.

Mrs. Naz came panting into the lunchroom and pried my fingers off Maryam's oily pigtail, and Maryam untangled herself. Maryam looked up at Mrs. Naz with large, wet eyes, then burst into tears. I stood to the side, eyes glinting with anger, spit shining on my chin, my clenched fist holding a clump of Maryam's coconut-oiled hair.

"Girls, what is happening? What is this? Are you animals or what?"

I jumped in quickly before blubbering Maryam could get a word in. "Madam, I acted in self-defense. Maryam said I wouldn't go to Heaven because my parents had a love marriage."

Mrs. Naz nodded. Straightened her shoulders. Then murmured, "Yes, a serious accusation indeed." She cleared her throat and asked loudly, "And did they?"

A hush fell over the girls.

Isn't it *You*, Allah, who decides three things for all Muslims—the day of birth, the day of death and the spouse one marries? *Even if* my parents did have a love marriage, then wouldn't it technically be *Your* fault? Why should *I* be punished for *Your* mistakes?

In a moment of madness or genius, I returned her gaze boldly, recklessly, and a question with three powerful words escaped my lips. "Madam, does it matter?"

The snicker brigade fanned out even further. "Devil-talk." "Such disrespect." "She is cursed." They whispered as they radiated out. Mrs. Naz furrowed her brow. "Mona Hasan, wipe that spittle off your chin and go see Principal Qadri right this instant. Such disregard for ... for ... *propriety* does not become a young lady endeavoring to come of age."

Ugh. How I hate it when Mrs. Naz admonishes us in confusing British English. Utterly dreadful. I turned my back on her and rolled my eyes out loud.

At the principal's office, I waited, tapping my toes while seated on the Bench of Shame. Principal Qadri finally came out of his office, holding a file folder with my name on it.

"Mona Hasan?"

I nodded.

"Ranking at top spot since grade one?"

I sat up and bobbled my head from side to side. This was my chance to inform Principal Qadri about the divisions in our class, about the new girl's attempts to dethrone me, her accusations on my good name, and on the good name of my father and mother! I was ready to spill it all. I drew in a sharp breath and opened my mouth. Before any words came out, Mr. Qadri spoke firmly and quickly. "Mona Hasan, don't do again whatever you were sent here for today. Back to class now," he instructed.

The hallway echoed with my footsteps as I made the slow, quiet walk back to my homeroom. Classes were already back in session, and I heard the scrape of chalk against the chalkboard. I stood outside the door of Room 6A. What to tell Mrs. Naz, who was in the middle of leading the class after lunch. Should I confess that Mr. Qadri didn't have time to give me a talking-to?

"Did you learn your lesson, Mona?" Mrs. Naz asked in a low voice when she saw me sulking by the door.

"Yes, I'm so very sorry, Mrs. Naz," I responded. She lifted her chin to signal that I could take my seat inside the classroom. I tucked my chin into my chest, feigning remorse, and slunk back to my seat. On the way, I stole a glance at Maryam.

She had rearranged her hair from a pigtail into a tight French braid that she had tucked into the nape of her neck:

something I wouldn't be able to yank. She looked at me with widened eyes and a mouth slightly agape—as if I was some kind of hideous monster—her eyes brimming with a mixture of disgust and fear.

Just so You know, Allah, the only lesson I learned today is that I must practice spitting.

Thursday, April 4, 1991

I came home from school seeing red. Ami was sitting on the sofa adding photos to a picture album. She was cross-legged, with sepia photographs surrounding her. Her tummy—rounding and obscene—was swelling against her clothes. I threw my backpack in the hallway and approached her angrily, my chin trembling.

"Who made your marriage?" I asked Ami loudly.

"*Made? My* marriage? Mona, what are you saying?"

"You've ruined my life! Did *you* make your own marriage?"

"Oh, Mona. Come sit with me and look at these pictures. I'll fix you a snack too, if you'd like."

I suppose this was as close to a confession as I would ever receive! What kind of mother makes her own ~~life~~ marriage?!

I cried all evening.

Saturday, April 6, 1991

After school, Ami came into my room and closed the door behind her. She took a deep breath and told me she had an important question to ask me. "Okay," I said and put down my sketch pad where I was doodling hearts over Waleed's name. She asked me if I liked being an older sister. "Of course not!" I replied quickly. An older sister's life is very difficult. Tutoo is always stealing my clothes and toys. If she makes a mess, both of us have to clean it up. If she cries or throws a tantrum, Ami gets cranky with both of us. If I get a new toy, nine and a half times out of ten, I have to share it with her. As far as I can see it, there have been no benefits in my life to having a younger sister, and I told all this to Ami quickly and clearly. I know Ami understood the sacrifices I make as an older sister because at the end of my ~~rant~~ speech, her chin wobbled and she left the room quickly!

Sunday, April 7, 1991

It. Bit. Bird poo.
You smell like my shoe.

I sing this song to Tutoo every time I need her to leave me alone.

Tutoo turns nine next month. She might be less annoying as a nine-year-old. She snuck into my room after school today demanding I play fairies with her! I relented on the condition that she do my math homework for me. Tutoo is a wiz at numbers. Everyone says so. Aba even says that Tutoo has the brains of a banker! It's too bad that she's a girl so she can never *be* a banker, but she could be a great math teacher one day.

Monday, April 8, 1991

Since it's Tutoo's birthday next month—well, to be exact, in thirty-three days, on the tenth of May—I've decided to gift Tutoo one of my own paintings for the occasion. It's very magnanimous—m-a-g-n-a-n-i-m-o-u-s—of me, as it will be worth quite a bit later in life.

I flipped through *Classic Paintings by the Masters* again, and this time I've decided to recreate my version of Claude Monet's *Terrasse à Sainte-Adresse*. I shall call it *Mona Hasan's La Corniche de Dubai*. It seems easy enough to pull off, and I'll just make some minor changes. The women will be in hijabs and the flags will be of the UAE and Pakistan . . . otherwise, it's basically the same scene, right?

Tuesday, April 9, 1991

I have decided that Tutoo and I should make up a dance routine to the bombastically brilliant Euro-rock pop song "The Final Countdown." This synthesizer smash-hit is sure to become a classic for the ages! We're going to perform the dance at her birthday party.

Tutoo wants us to dance to a super-slow one-hit wonder, "Imagine," by somebody called John Lemon, but that piano blister is a SNOOZE-FEST of a song! It's super sluggish, and then our dance will be so dull! We need a faster song for the twirls, turns and jumps I have in mind. Also, the song I've chosen is my secret message to the world. I know that if I keep praying, then Mrs. Naz will open the gym doors. This song is a countdown to the day of love that I know is just around the corner!

Wednesday, April 10, 1991

Tutoo's such a klutz. She keeps messing up my routine. But she has to be my partner, as I can't boss anyone else around half this much. She says she wouldn't make so many mistakes if the song was slower, like that icky-sicky slow song by John Linen.

Thursday, April 11, 1991

According to Hala, secondhand bookstores in Cairo have secret shelves and backrooms huffing and puffing with all the books that you can't find easily here in the UAE. *Any* Cairo book-wallah can find you *any* book on *any* topic. If you want to read about all the wives that Prophet Muhammad had (more than four, Hala says), then you'll find that book in Cairo. And if you really want to know about the history of fighting between Iraq and Kuwait, or the history of tongue-kissing, or how retaliation begins and how it could end, or how to write the best love poetry to make anyone fall in love with you, then you'll find all that inside a Cairo bookstore too.

Hala brought a knapsack of books from Cairo that we can't find easily in the UAE. She says she is going to sell them and make lots of money on the black market. She just needs to find the proper improper buyers.

She showed us some of the books. They were by authors we had never heard of—writers writing in Arabic, like Nawal El Saadawi and Naguib Mahfouz, and others writing in Urdu, like Fahmida Riaz and Ismat Chughtai. She held each dusty, torn paperback like it was a jewel dropped from Heaven. "They won't teach you these books at school," Hala bragged. Then she fished out a children's book from the bottom of her bag. It had originally been written in Dutch and later translated into English. "A thirteen-year-old wrote this," Hala said and slid it toward me. I reached out and saw the words *Diary* and *Frank*, but then Hala changed her mind and swiftly grabbed the book back. "No, wait, this one is real. This one is going to fetch me top dirhams." She tossed me two others instead, but my mind rattled with the one she'd taken away.

Who is Anne Frank, Allah?

Friday, April 12, 1991

One of the books Hala gave me yesterday is called *The Secret Diary of Adrian Mole, Aged 13¾*, and it's about a thirteen-year-old boy growing up in a part of England called the "East Midlands," which sounds a lot like the "Middle East," doesn't it, and I think I'll like this book! I've already sped through the first chunk of it. I've never been to England, and I don't know any boys from England, so it's really interesting to learn about how self-centered and comically clueless they can be.

Saturday, April 13, 1991

After school. Aba came into my room and asked me whether I would like a baby sister or brother. I said neither. Why do my parents keep yammering on and on about another sibling? I hope they aren't thinking about adopting one of the Iraqi orphans on TV.

Before bedtime. After dinner, Aba announced that Ami is pregnant! *Our* mother!!!!!!!!!!!!!!!

Now Tutoo and I will be laughingstocks at school. How could our parents do this to us in their old age?

Aba announced the news very casually. He said, matter-of-factly, "By the way, girls, your mother is pregnant, so I expect you to help out around the house more."

HELP around the house?! What about the solitude and serenity needed for my burgeoning—b-u-r-g-e-o-n-i-n-g—Poetry career? How can I possibly achieve fame and riches as a Poetess if I am to be saddled with older sister responsibilities! How can I properly ponder word choices, metaphors and rhymes if there's a baby stinking the place up around me? I will have to do my very best not to let the new Attention-Hogger ruin my life.

When my mother came in to say goodnight, I gave her a kiss on both cheeks. She asked, "Are you pleased about the baby, Mona?" I lied and said yes.

I hope Ami doesn't think I'm going to help change its diapers or rock the monster to sleep.

Sunday, April 14, 1991

Guess who?

Uncle Annoying, that's who!

He hasn't been around for a while, but he said he won't be able to make it to Tutoo's birthday party next month and wanted to drop off a birthday present for her. He bought her a trio of stubby little dolls with brightly colored hair (they are called "trolls" and, after the Cabbage Patch dolls, they are the Must-Have Doll for nine-year-olds this year). As a pity gift for being *sister-of*-birthday-girl, Uncle Annoying had something for me too—a poster of the Teenage Mutant Ninja Turtles. How old does he think I am?

He went on and on about how Tutoo's becoming such a big girl now and gave her a tinned box of chocolates too. I saw Tutoo ballooning with pride again.

!!!!!!!!!

After he left, I marched over to Ami, who had been busy in the kitchen making round balls of kofta, or meatball, for a curry, and told her that Uncle Annoying was far too annoying, and that old uncles shouldn't be so gross and give attention to young girls like Tutoo, and that he needed to find friends his own age. Ami fixed me with a disapproving look. "Mona, he's just being friendly. Quiet. What will people say?" I felt like I was looking at a stranger and my face shifted from confusion to anger, and it made Ami's face flush.

I sighed loudly and my mother sighed loudly, and I grabbed Tutoo by the arm, took her into my bedroom and locked the door behind us. I told Tutoo that the attention an older man gives a younger girl is fraught with risk and danger and is about the control an older man wants over a younger girl. I reminded Tutoo about the creepy men we see out in the streets who we don't know. In taxis. In buses. In malls. In video stores. Like the ones who look at young girls up and down, screaming bad things with their eyes. The ones who wet their lips, sing naughty songs, make bad noises. Who whistle *even when*, or *especially when*, girls are walking by fast, heads down.

I told her that I had flipped back and forth between a thesaurus and a dictionary and found a word for this kind of behavior, and it was called manipulation—m-a-n-i-p-u-l-a-t-i-o-n.

Then we threw out his candy together.

Tuesday, April 16, 1991

The last few days of Ramadan passed by in a whirl as they always do. So much cumin and cardamom and saffron simmering or steeping or soaking in bowls and pots, and so many dates and pomegranates and almonds and pistachios to pick off! But finally Ramadan is over and today is Eid! Eid ul Fitr, the "Feast for Breaking Fasts." My parents call this Eid the "Choti Eid" (the small Eid) or "Meethi Eid" (the Eid with sweets), and I like this one more than the other Eid, Eid ul Adha, or as I sometimes call it, the "Feast for Ibrahim's Sacrifice," which will come later this summer.

The important thing about this Eid is that it's been falling on the school year for the past few years (thank you, lunar calendar!), and I get to be off school for three days.

Tutoo and I scrubbed ourselves red and raw in the shower early this morning, then dressed ourselves in our brand-new, itchy shalwar kameez. We ran to the dining table, where we elbowed each other to get first dibs on our favorite dishes that our mother had spent the night preparing. Sheer korma—condensed milk pudding with pistachios, cloves and raisins; sheermal—sweet flatbread with ghee, sugar and saffron milk; phirni—a thick, creamy pudding with ground rice, nuts, rose petals and fruit; gajar ka halwa—semolina cooked with carrots, milk, almonds, sugar, butter and cardamom. We stuffed ourselves until bursting point, then laid down our prayer mats and made our Eid prayers at home with our parents. We moaned and groaned from standing to kneeling and back again. At the end of Eid prayers, when it was time to make duas, I was selfish. I could have wished for world peace or a safe pregnancy for my mother or for Uncle Annoying to blow up, but instead, now that Ramadan was over, I wished to see Waleed again. For a moment, I felt good. A moment after, I felt guilty about feeling good. The moment after the after, I felt good about feeling guilty about feeling good. Then I began to feel dizzy and got off the prayer mat.

By late afternoon, guests started to pour in and out for Eid greeting and gifting and feasting. Ami had already told us earlier that Uncle Annoying wouldn't be among the guests, but Tutoo and I remained glued together, side by side in attack position, anyway. I was disappointed not to see him, but Tutoo looked relieved. Tutoo and I hugged our guests, bellowed "Eid Mubarak" and pocketed soft, lumpy envelopes of cash—our Eidi. Tutoo and I agreed we should donate this year's Eidi to a charity that helps girls and women.

Wednesday, April 17, 1991

Second day of the three days of Eid greeting and gifting and feasting. This time we were visitors at other people's homes, to gorge on their home-cooked goodies. Everywhere we went, the tables were laden with heavy dishes, and table legs were perilously close to buckling.

Thursday, April 18, 1991

Ami's friend Neighbor Auntie is Hindu. Her husband passed away when she was quite young. She lives in one of the smallest apartments, a few floors below us. She has a white cat with a black tail that she calls "Rat" (the cat, not the tail). Her place is cramped but cozy and her smiles always reach up to her eyes.

Tutoo and I are allowed to go over and cuddle her cat as much as we want or play with the jewelry she keeps in shoeboxes under her bed. We always pay her a visit during Eid, not only because she gets a bit bored (she is a Hindu, after all), but also because she cooks the best non-meat dishes in the building. Today she made fluffy, steamed rice and lentil cakes called idli to go with sambar, a hot lentil soup with tamarind, diced okra and eggplant. She also made fresh uttapam for us, which are a type of South Indian pancake made with tomatoes, onions, chilies, grated carrots and beets. As side dishes, she made three different kinds of chutney from super-secret recipes handed down to her from her mother— mint, mango and coconut. We also downed two glasses of a tasty drink she made with nunnari roots, herbs and lime called "nunnari sherbet." Okay, so a whole lot of vegetables in your food may sound like a funny thing to get excited about, but as Neighbor Auntie always tells us, "If someone hasn't had vegetables prepared the Tamil way, then they haven't had vegetables!" Tutoo and I ate and ate until our ears were about to pop off.

But even with all this deliciousness, Neighbor Auntie's dining table isn't my favorite space in her home. My favorite space is a corner in her living room where she's wedged a little bookshelf. This little bookshelf is her puja, or worship area. On the top shelf, there are four Hindu god statues and one Hindu god in a framed painting. There's a Ganesh statue, with his elephant head. And in the back is a statue of Nataraja, the cosmic dancer, balancing on one foot in an elegant posture and fanning his four arms delicately. My favorite is the little statue of Durga Maa sitting on a lion with one knee bent. She's got eight arms and each arm is holding a different weapon to create or destroy. A blue-bodied Vishnu stands regally, looking out serenely from a tiny painting within a gold frame. And next to him is a statue of Hanuman, the monkey god, with his tail proudly sticking up from behind his human body.

I know, I know. Animal faces and tails on human bodies? Human bodies with more than two arms? Tutoo once asked Neighbor Auntie how she could possibly pray to gods who . . . well . . . *You* know. But Tutoo didn't want to hurt her feelings, so she left the rest unsaid. Neighbor Auntie shrugged her shoulders and answered that for her, gods weren't actual creatures; for her, gods were necessary *dreams* of creatures. That she prayed not *to* gods, but *for* gods, because life was often difficult and exhausting and scary.

Foolish, right? I know not to pray *to* You or *for* You. Prayer is obviously for things *from* You.

Tuesday, April 23, 1991

Eid holidays are over and we've been back to school for about ten days now. Maryam and the Full Socks have steered clear of Laila and me, and we have steered clear of them. The only new development is that Laila has started to dress like a goth after school. This is lamentable but understandable given how long Laila's mother has been working outside the home. Despite her egregious—e-g-r-e-g-i-o-u-s—fashion choices, I remain Laila's steadfast and loyal friend.

Sunday, April 28, 1991

We finally had our first gym class after Eid holidays, and Waleed walked by with a big smile and his hands cupped together in a heart shape! His smile shone like a beacon from a lighthouse and filled me with warmth.

> **Waleed of Dubai by Mona Hasan, 11¼**
> Oh, what a sight!
> My heart flew like a kite
> When walked by my heart's true delight.

It's been far too long! Time to figure out date number two.

CHAPTER FIVE

May

Wednesday, May 1, 1991

Halfway through gym class, my heart started pounding a mile a minute. I excused myself and walked over to where Mrs. Naz was standing by the gym door.

"I need a washroom pass," I told her.

"You can wait until class is over," she said.

I looked her straight in the eye. "It's a tricky time of the month."

She let out a loud sigh. Tilted her head to the side. Imagined herself on another planet. "Okay, I've got my eye on the clock. You have five minutes," she said.

Five minutes would be enough. I walked out to the hall and let the door shut behind me. After the door clicked in place, I started a full-on sprint. Down the hall. Across the blazing field. Back into the girls' building. Into the main hall. Down the quiet corridor toward the principal's office. Nobody was around. It was now or never.

I turned the corner into an empty stairwell. By this time, two minutes and forty seconds had passed. I stood there as my heart hammered loudly and I stared at the little red box on the wall. This was the only thing that separated me from what I wanted.

5 . . .

4 . . .

3 . . .

2 . . .

1!

I flipped the glass case up. Grasped the red handle inside. Then I did it. I pulled the fire alarm.

WEE-WAH. WEE-WAH. WEE-WAH. WEE-WAH. WEE-WAH. WEE-WAH.

Maybe the cost of the life I wanted would be a broken ear! As the alarm rang out in a million decibels, I sprinted back toward the boys' section. The plan was to get back before Mrs. Naz would have everyone lined up outside on the field. I meant to dash to the washroom and emerge as if I'd just finished my business. But by the time I got to the boys' building, there was a stampede of teachers and students pouring out of classrooms and library rooms and gym rooms. Everyone was fanning out in every possible direction, and I blended into the crowd.

Mr. Qadri's panicked voice trilled over the alarm—"Attention! Attention!! Attention, everyone!!! The fire trucks are on their way. Teachers and students—there is no need to PANIC! PANIC will not be helpful. Students, follow your teachers to the nearest exits and gather on the field. Remember, there is no need to PANIC! I repeat, do not PANIC!!!"

It appeared the whole world was out on the field! No one was organized into neat rows. Instead the students gathered in messy groups, and the teachers scrambled about, flustered.

I walked over to Waleed.

"Oooooooooooh!" Waleed's friends teased as they saw me walk up.

"Smoochie, smoochie!" The grade-eight boys puckered their lips and swiveled their hips. Were they trying to embarrass him or me? Or themselves?

Waleed and I walked off to a quiet part of the field. He stuttered through some love poetry, and I batted my eyes up at him. *Kiss me, you fool*, I messaged him via my silent brain powers. At the end of his poem, I softly murmured, "Brilliant! Brilliant!" then cleared my throat impatiently. A look of hurt and horror washed over his face. He sniffed. "I'm not at the end yet. Is something stuck in your throat?"

Only Cupid's arrow, I conjectured to myself. To Waleed, I presented a sheepish smile and responded, "Oh, some desert sand, perhaps." I scratched at my throat and resumed listening. Wide-eyed. Doe-eyed. *Hope*-eyed. He resumed stuttering.

The fire alarms continued to ring around us and probably interfered with the messages I was sending him in my head. I grew impatient and reached out for his hand. But due to unfortunate positioning and timing, my hand almost hit his dingle-dangle. We both jumped back as if we'd been branded by fire and mutely rejoined our classmates out on the field.

Thursday, May 2, 1991

What fools love makes of us all! I can't believe I pulled the fire alarm yesterday and caused so much chaos. I feel guilty about creating all that mayhem, but thankfully not guilty enough—besides, the experience has given me a few new ideas about how to meet up again. One must risk it all for love!

> **Lovesick by Mona Hasan, 11½**
> What madness love drives one to!
> I lied and said I needed to go to the loo.
> Instead I pulled the fire alarm and it went wee-
> woo.
> I wanted to hold his hand but almost touched
> his dingle-doo.
> This poem is not very poetic, so what to do—
> I'll end on a line that is irrefutable and true:
> Waleed, I love thee as much as I love chocolate
> fondue!

Friday, May 3, 1991

HOLIDAY today, so Aba dropped off Ami, Tutoo and me at the women-only beach. This is where all the haram-shaped women go to enjoy the beach and relax without men ogling them. In this way, we only have to contend with the ogling women. Tutoo and I spit watermelon seeds into the sea to see whose would go farthest. Aba came to pick us up and on the drive back home, Tutoo was so upset that I won the watermelon-seed game that she wouldn't let me look out her window until I screamed and threw a fit for twenty minutes. Older sisters have the toughest life. It's terrible.

Saturday, May 4, 1991

Being the firstborn comes with many drawbacks. One of the biggest is having to share your precious belongings with the ~~gremlins~~ younger siblings in your home. There's a lot of whining and complaining, and if you make the mistake of capitulating, then you have to listen to *their* whining and wheedling too! There's also the damage your siblings do to your possessions, which means that you might not even want your things returned anymore! I could go on and on about my hardships and privations—p-r-i-v-a-t-i-o-n-s. I was reminded of this struggle today when Tutoo returned the paint supplies I'd lent her last week. The paintbrushes had flecks of dry paint in them, and misshapen bristles! Completely ruined. I suppose the one saving grace is that right now I only have a *single* sibling to contend with and I should enjoy this calm before the storm as much as possible! Most of my classmates have been subjected to a duo or a trio since birth, and some have even had a quartet foisted upon them.

Wednesday, May 8, 1991

Today when the bell for lunchtime rang, Tutoo bolted toward me. We haven't been talking for the last few days given our watermelon-seed fight, but I'm happy to report that she finally caved!

"Let's put our argument about the watermelon seeds behind us, Baji," she said and tugged me by the hand, leading me into the little-kid yard. We drew animals in her sketchbook under the olive tree. While she sharpened the pencils I wanted, I looked up at her face, as she was hard at work trimming the pencil tips into fine points, and I realized that the perfect number of sisters to have is one. This very one.

Having a little sister who loves me so much that she wants to be just like me is possibly not the worst thing on this planet. Even if she steals my toys and shoes and origami swans.

Tutoo's always been there for me. I mean, she's my sister, so of course she's always been around, but what I also realized today is that her devotion to me is constant. Unconditional. And that it's a useful burden after all.

If Tutoo wasn't around, how would I know that no matter what I'll always be smarter and prettier than somebody else in this world?

Thursday, May 9, 1991

Tutoo's birthday party is TOMORROW, so Tutoo and I spent the evening practicing our dance performance. It's almost ready. Our grand debut is just a day away. *Toes and fingers crossed!* Tutoo better not mess this up!

Friday, May 10, 1991

I woke Tutoo up early in the morning by singing her a song—

> *Happy birthday to you,*
> *happy birthday to you,*
> *You look like a wombat and smell like its poo!*
> *Happy birthday to you!*

Ami made Tutoo a cake in the shape of a cat. Ami's never made an animal cake for any of *my* birthdays! When the guests poured in, we played Musical Chairs, Pass the Parcel and Simon Says. Before we cut the cake and blew out the candles, Tutoo and I arranged our guests in a semicircle in the living room and shushed them. Then we dimmed the lights. Tutoo and I began our Grand Dance.

Sure enough, in the middle of our routine Tutoo had a big fat fall, but because she dusted herself off and got back up, grinning, and rejoined the routine, the grown-ups gave her extra-loud applause and pats on the back! Neighbor Auntie even made the *ulululu* sound. I didn't make a single mistake but no one congratulated me on my perfection. No one was even looking at me! Everyone's eyes were on the birthday girl.

Tutoo looked elated. She received a mini-mountain of gifts. No one gifted me anything at all and my birthday isn't until the end of October! Tutoo said she would share her gifts with me, but it's not the same as being the one in charge of doing all the sharing.

On top of all this, Neighbor Auntie gifted Tutoo a Gift from Overseas, and it got a lot of oohs and aahs. A Cabbage Patch doll! Her name is Tabitha and she has yellow hair in two braids. You can't buy Cabbage Patch dolls anywhere in Dubai! Neighbor Auntie bought the gift when she visited London earlier this year. Even though I'll be turning twelve later this year and will be much too sophisticated for dolls, Neighbor Auntie better get me one for my birthday too!

Wednesday, May 15, 1991

Still mulling over all the presents Tutoo received on her birthday!

The thing is, if I didn't have a sister, I would have much more of my parents' attention and many more toys. Ami would gift me her party saris, and all her beautiful Mughal-inspired Indian jewelry would be mine too.

I would be the only queen in the hive!

It's not at all fair that every year Tutoo has a birthday before mine.

Thursday, May 16, 1991

Uncle Annoying invited himself over for a slice of leftover birthday cake this evening. I heard my mother try to make an excuse but ultimately she was inept and gave in. "Of course, a short visit this evening should be fine," she said weakly.

I wanted to keep him away from Tutoo, so I took him to see where I had hung the Teenage Mutant Ninja Turtle poster he'd gifted me on Tutoo's birthday. He stood behind me while I showed him the poster that I had taped on the wall in my bedroom. Sure, TMNT are much too jejune— j-e-j-u-n-e—for me, but I still put it up with the others. One side of my wall is plastered with pictures. I have movie posters of Star Wars, *The Princess Bride* and *The Goonies*. I also have famous-people posters of timeless legends like David Hasselhoff, Rick Astley, the two guys from *Miami Vice*, Leonardo DiCaprio and the New Kids on the Block. I've also taped up the two kings of Bollywood cinema— Salman and Aamir Khan. I rambled on and on about my favorites to Uncle Annoying and felt my bra strap slide off my right shoulder. Darn thing was loose! Uncle Annoying reached out to slide it back in place. It was pretty high on the Slimeball-O-Meter, and I was just getting ready to stomp my right heel on his hairy toes, but then Ami walked in out of nowhere and his hands fell to his sides. Ami narrowed her eyes at Uncle Annoying. "Your wife just called." She frowned. "It's time for you to leave."

!!!

Even I know that asking a guest to leave your home is at the very top of the list of super-rude things to do, but in this case it was a CNS (Critical and Necessary Situation).

After he left, my mother let out a long exhalation. "Mona, I was wrong about Uncle Annoying . . . and I was very wrong about wondering what other people might think. I'm glad you listened to yourself," she conceded. I knew that this meant one thing for sure—an extra scoop of ice cream and as many drizzles of chocolate syrup as I could squeeze out tonight!

But what I wasn't sure about was what would happen to Uncle Annoying now, and I asked my mother. She replied tiredly but firmly, "Leave that part up to your father and me, but you can be sure that you won't see him again."

Friday, May 17, 1991

When a bad thing is happening, parents think the best thing to do is not talk about it. Everyone is too scared to mention the elephant in the room, the annoying uncle or the war on the horizon. They think that if they talk to us directly and openly about the bad thing (that has happened or is happening or will happen), that somehow the bad thing will get bigger. Expand. Instead, they don't see that conversation could lighten the load, turn the elephant into a butterfly, build a path toward peace. The bad thing never needs to go away (and really, if a bad thing is out to get you or someone you love, then nothing can make it go away), but the *fear* around and about the bad thing, well, that needs a chance to shrink, doesn't it, and talking about it IS the only way *through* it, right?

Ami could have made the situation with Uncle Annoying so much easier if she had just listened to me a month ago! But sometimes grown-ups aren't the heroes we need them to be, which is really sad. Sometimes we have to put the superhero cloak on ourselves.

Saturday, May 18, 1991

I spent the time after school by Tutoo's side. We colored unicorns and kittens in her favorite coloring book, and I even let her show me how to make an alligator out of an old egg carton. She did a kooky interpretive-type dance to "Imagine" by that John Lentil singer, and I applauded her loudly, maybe even threw in an *ulululu*. We ended the evening by rewatching *Aliens*. I sat by her side and held her hand tightly. I pointed at the screen. "Look. Look closely. We don't have to play nice. Look at where anger can take us."

Sunday, May 19, 1991

After school today, I threw off my backpack and climbed into a long, low cardboard box with Tutoo, which we played with for two hours. We rowed our peanut-colored cardboard ship through stormy seas. We hung long-limbed stuffies around our necks and pretended we were mariners of yore. We took lines from a Coleridge poem and created our own English-Urdu mishmash to suit our game better. "Paani, paani everywhere, but not a drop to drink anywhere!" we moaned as we stumbled around our playroom, feeling dehydrated and doomed. Then we took a break for mango lassis and samosas, and returned to beat back a gang of loathsome pirates and row toward land with our tennis rackets.

After an afternoon of Ship-Ship, Tutoo and I played Narnia-Narnia. We scooped all our shoes and clothes out of our closet and threw them all into a giant pile on the floor. Then we climbed into the bottom of the closet. We shut the doors from inside and squeezed our eyes shut. In the darkness, we interlaced our fingers and held our breath. We did countdowns out loud, hoping to open our eyes in faraway lands with talking animals and other treasures. Each time our eyes fluttered open, we found ourselves trapped in this same inadequate world, but we shut our eyes and tried over and over anyway.

Even though Tutoo's a full three grades younger, I'd forgotten how much fun it is to play with someone who still believes in magic.

Wednesday, May 22, 1991

Tutoo made me a thank-you card for the painting I made for her birthday. Inside, she wrote out all the words to her favorite warble-whine of a song, "Imagine" by John Lion.

On the back of the card, she added a handwritten note: "You are my worst foe and my bestest friend. You are my sun and my moon. For my birthday, I want to be just like you."

Who wouldn't?!

But I think I've completed my good-sister duties for the year, and Tutoo needs to remember her place as the bratty little shrimp she is and not bother me too often. I have grandiose poems to create, after all! Witness my latest—

> **Control by Mona Hasan, 11½**
> He wanted to control my sister because he was
> a bum.
> Oh, what a lousy scum!
> My mother should have beat him like a drum.

Friday, May 24, 1991

It's FRIDAY today, so the parents took us to Safa Park along Al Wasl Road.

Safa Park is a very fun but sad place to visit. Aba told us that it used to be a home for Dubai's poor workers. These poor workers or laborers worked very hard but were not paid for it. They couldn't get paid what they were owed as they had passport problems or what's called *legal* problems. They lived quietly in Safa Park, trying to make enough to eat, and at first no one bothered them because Safa Park used to be a large garbage area with no running water or electricity. Aba always says that this country was built off, and continues to be built off, the sweat of poor laborers.

But at some point, the Dubai government bulldozed their homes and made an amusement park. Now Safa Park has playgrounds, a Ferris wheel, a maze and a bumper car area. A big problem is that the playground's slides heat up like knives in the heat. A bigger problem is that it doesn't seem fair that those people were just trying to make a home and weren't bothering anyone, and why can't we just share the unimportant stuff (like land) with everyone, and keep the important stuff (like love notes folded into origami shapes) for ourselves?

Wednesday, May 29, 1991

I am suffering in abject agony, pining away for my One True Love, but there is nonstop misery at home too. Today my mother was tired from creating a baby all day! This meant I had to do all her housework. There were an awful lot of things to do! All this time, I had thought being a mother meant soap operas and afternoon naps. Alas, not so.

This mountain of housework boggles my mind, Allah.

How have men put a man on the moon but haven't yet built machines to help women with all their women work? In the movie *Aliens*, Ripley could only have beaten up the bad aliens in outer space. On earth, she'd have had no time to fight.

CHAPTER SIX

June

Saturday, June 1, 1991

BREAKING NEWS!!!

We

Are

M O V I N G ! ! !

T O   C A N A D A ! ! !

Yes, it's terrible news, but our parents have decided to get along and now they both agree that it IS the right time for doing that immigration thing after all. Aba told Tutoo and me that our passports right now tell the world we are from Pakistan but he's going to buy new ones for us that say we are from Canada!

CANADA!

I just can't believe it!

C A N A D A!

Our parents told us that the paperwork has been filled out and mailed in, and that we will be in Canada by the end of the summer!

Why are our parents ruining our lives by moving us to Canada, Allah?

"There's a new baby on the way, and it's a chance for a new beginning, and it'll be exciting and marvelous, and we have an opportunity to live a brand-new life and blah, blah, blah."

Tutoo and I pressed Aba on why he was ripping us away from the only home we had ever known! He steepled his fingers together and offered, "'*One must explore to see,*' na?" Neither of our parents have actually been to Canada before! They have one distant relative—a second cousin of a second cousin—who moved there twenty years ago and that's it! They also don't have a clue *which* city in Canada we should move to! All they know is that the country sits on top of America, and it is cold. It seems ~~a tad foolish~~ completely absurd to dive into such a gargantuan life decision with so few details figured out! But our parents seem to blindly believe that moving to Canada will mean a better future for all of us!

Ami said she wrote a letter to her parents last week informing them of our move. Ami speaks to them as little as possible, so that means our parents must really be serious about leaving!!!!

Sunday, June 2, 1991

I gave Laila the Bad News over the phone: "My parents have decided to pay money to Canada for new passports and soon we'll be leaving for our New Life in a New World." I was nervous. What if she wasn't as sad about my leaving as I wanted her to be? *Needed* her to be?

Laila arrived at our front door fifteen minutes later, breathless and distraught.

"Woe to me, Mona—I will never again find a friend as magnificent as you." Laila's eyes welled up as she continued, "I promise it, Mona Hasan. If another student so much as looks at me, I shall turn my head and turn up my nose. After you have moved to the Land of Snow and Ice, I shall refuse to smile or laugh, and I shall sit alone for all of my lunchtimes. You shall remain my truest and only best friend for all of my days!"

This was an adequate reaction to the news of my imminent move dislocation, and we hugged, held hands and cried as miserably as we could.

My best friend shall yearn and long for me forever, won't she, Allah?

Monday, June 3, 1991

Laila and I can't think of a single thing Canada is famous for! An ice storm? A famous igloo, maybe? Any movies set in

Canada? Are there even any good-looking actors that live in Canada, Allah?

We have heard from multiple sources that the sidewalks in America are paved with gold. Sheikhs in Dubai have toilets made of gold, but golden sidewalks sound pretty okay too, don't they? Since Canada is right next to America, Laila and I hope that Canadian sidewalks will be dusted with gold flakes (at the bare minimum)! I have promised to write Laila from Canada and vowed to send her some gold flakes in my first letter.

Tuesday, June 4, 1991

My mother received a reply from her parents! The letter came in an oblong white envelope with a blue border. I noticed she crumpled up the letter and threw it in the kitchen garbage. I fished it out and took it to my room to copy its contents into my diary:

Dearest Shireen,

As-salamu alaikum wa-rahmatu-llahi wa-barakatuh.

Your father and I are very sorry to hear about your immigration plans for Canada. There is still time to change your mind and consider instead a return to the Safe-Haven-for-Sunni-Muslims-in-a-certain-income-bracket-and-of-a-certain-lineage that is your birth country, Pakistan.

While it is true that we never did agree to your impetuous marriage to Haider (being that his family is not of the same pure blood as ours, and in at least four generations of our illustrious family, no one has dared to marry someone from across the river), that is mostly behind us now. You cannot deny that the hasty marriage was a scandalous choice on your part, but we magnanimously decided not to ostracize you and, as mentioned, that is mostly behind us now.

We are thrilled that you are with child at your advanced age. We pray that this time around, you will be blessed with a male child, since as we all know, this will go some distance in rectifying your current status as a woman of questionable repute.

If you had put your faith in Allah, Shireen, then he would not have visited war so close to the UAE, as Allah only punishes the pleasure-seekers and the kafirs. We were saddened to hear through various sources that alcohol was consumed at your house during a celebration on December 31, 1990. As you are well aware, the Gregorian calendar is full of inaccuracies and filth. You weren't brought up to enjoy life like this, Shireen. What sort of message is this for your daughters? Live as you want? Love as you desire? History has taught us that these are scandalous, nay, pernicious ideas for young people in general, and young girls in particular. You have been tempting Allah's wrath with your ways for far too long, Shireen. Come to your senses and return to Pakistan so that we may enclose you in love and judgment.

We also wish to inform you that your father and I are going on Hajj in a few months to pray for the pardon of your pleasure-seeking soul. We will put in a special request that your sojourn to the Land of the Infidels is short, and we look forward to embracing you once again in our warm bosom and lovingly whispering, "I told you so."

With warmest affection and with enclosed stickers for your girl children,

Your Elder Mother, Nanijaan, and Elder Father, Nanajaan

Wednesday, June 5, 1991

Ami has not sat down to pen a reply to her parents yet, and I haven't said anything to her about it either. She is bound to have many such moments of blunder, given the stresses of her pregnancy.

Thursday, June 6, 1991

MORE BREAKING NEWS IN THE YEAR OF BREAKING NEWS!!

Our parents just told Tutoo and me that we are going on a trip to the "Motherland" (according to Ami and Aba, this means the country of Pakistan). This is because Aba needs to give the immigration news to his mother in person. "I am my mother's favorite child, after all, and I must find the perfect golden moment to break her heart delicately," he explained, and he warned us not to blab the news ourselves. We haven't been to Pakistan for two full summers (our aunts and uncles usually visit us instead)! Last year Aba's friend from work got married in Egypt, so we flew to Cairo and made a summer vacation out of it. We saw the pyramids of Giza. Rode camels in the desert. Floated down the Nile on a boat. Spent hours roaming Cairo's National Museum (where I cross-my-heart-hope-to-die-put-a-needle-in-my-eye swear I didn't pocket a single coin, pebble, brick or papyrus fragment, even though it would have been so very easy). We also visited restaurants in Zamalek, took pictures in Old Cairo, and met up with Laila and her family at their second home in Heliopolis, where we played with their pet poodle, Ramses. We stuffed ourselves on her mother's home cooking, and Tutoo and I plucked all the petals off the flower bushes in their large garden and hid them in our pockets. We learned how ancient Egyptians made papyrus and perfume, and wandered Khan el-Khalili souk, an outdoor market, eating roasted peanuts and haggling for silver trinkets. It was a *proper* summer vacation—being foreigners in a *foreign* land!

We did the same thing the year before, when we took a summer vacation to neighboring Oman. Aba mapped out a three-week road trip where we explored dusty small towns and learned about Bedouin history and culture. Oman was completely unlike Dubai—mountains and sand dunes and ravines, wildlife and plant life and warmth and hospitality and smiling faces everywhere! We took boat rides on the water-flooded wadis, or valleys, and sat atop baying donkeys as they took us through beautiful canyons. We wandered souks, looking at handmade Omani jewelry during the day, and during the night, we saw doles of rare turtles retreat into the glittering Arabian Sea.

Alas, this year our parents want us to have none of the wonder and awe of a *proper* summer vacation! Instead they want to take us back "home" to spend time with our grandparents and aunts and uncles and cousins in sweaty, sticky Pakistan—*unbelievable.* Now we'll have to spend this miserable summer being foreigners in a *familiar* land!

My parents were born in Pakistan but came to the UAE as soon as they got married, and Tutoo and I were born in the UAE! I'm not sure why our parents feel that Pakistan is *their* Motherland, nor at all sure why they feel that it should be *ours.*

We will spend most of our time with Aba's family in the capital city of Islamabad, like we always do, and we'll make a short trip to see Ami's family, who live in the posh part of the city.

Friday, June 7, 1991

FRIDAY today, so the parents took us to Al Nasr Leisure-land. Tutoo and I played on the banana swings and pineapple slides and bumper cars. The only problem was that it was hotter than jalapeño underwear, so Aba asked us if we wanted to try ice-skating instead. He meant to excite us by regaling us with tales of Canada being full of frost and ice, cascading snow and glittering frozen lakes, but when we looked at the hard ice and sharp blades, it had the opposite effect. Tail-bruising falls on cold, hard ice? We adamantly shook our heads "no"—what kind of barbarians did this for fun? We'd much rather be at the beach, so we made our way over there instead.

Saturday, June 8, 1991

We leave for our summer vacation to Pakistan tomorrow. School isn't going to be over for another few weeks, but thankfully our teachers never mind if we leave for summer vacation early to visit families back "home." Ami tells us that they're so understanding because they would love a chance to do the same.

Today was my last day of school, so through a series of notes, Waleed and I arranged to have a fifteen-minute private meeting in an empty classroom in the middle of the afternoon. Our farewell was miserable and tearful. This was because Waleed had penned a long epic on the occasion of our parting, and I was subjected to a lengthy recitation. My insides twisted but I listened with the utmost patience, only to be rewarded at the denouement with a chaste peck on the cheek! Waleed seemed quite pleased with himself for having the courage to do so, but I was despondent and frankly inconsolable. Nevertheless, I swallowed my disappointment and promised that I would wait for him until he found a way to get to Canada. I assured him that I would refrain from falling in love with the good-looking Canadians that I was sure to be surrounded by, and he swore to do the same with the riff-raff here. I didn't need a teary goodbye at school with Laila, as we are going to be pen pals for life.

I told Laila that when we get to Islamabad, we will be staying with my father's side of the family since my mother tries to avoid her family as much as she can. Laila lamented with me that this was a shame and a great injustice, as on my father's side of the family, there is no AC.

Sunday, June 9, 1991

The plane ride lasted weeks and weeks! Ami said it was three and a half hours.

We landed in Islamabad in the middle of the day. Islamabad is Pakistan's capital city. My cousins call it "Isloo."

It was 2:00 p.m. and already thirty-eight degrees! Dubai has tons of air conditioners that operate at full-blast everywhere, but Isloo has none. Dubai has shiny towers and bright lights. Isloo just has lush trees and flowers—*YUCK*.

After we got off our flight, we had to wait half an hour in the sticky heat for Aba's family to come pick us up, as they are always running late. We saw our grandmother come shuffling over to hug us first. Then our aunts, uncles and cousins lunged at us joyfully. Dadi's next door neighbor, Next-Door Uncle, had come with his two kids too. He ruffled our hair, pinched our cheeks and threw Tutoo in the air, but he didn't count as a family member—we just needed his minivan to fit everyone in.

Monday, June 10, 1991

It's been two summers since I was last in Isloo. Isloo still has peddlers selling vegetables in wooden carts, going up and down the street announcing deals and discounts in one breathless scream. The donkeys pulling their wagons still bray much too loudly. The bicycle vendors crying out their services—selling corn, sharpening knives, fixing gas stoves and water heaters, mending fabric, buying up old newspapers and bits and pieces of metal—still have their shrill songs, and colorful Pakistani trucks still honk at all hours impatiently. And if any of this wasn't enough, Next-Door Uncle's rooster has only grown bigger and bolder, and it was sure to let us all know that at the crack of dawn this morning. Oh, and did I mention the nonstop chatter, or gup-shup, inside our Dadi's house? Our uncles and aunties and their children are a torrent of opinion and gossip and rumors and political news and jokes and teasing and unsolicited advice and love and love and so much love. The affection between my father and his siblings is a feeling so thick that you could pluck it from the air and plop it into your mouth. The problem is that everyone has a lot to say and always all at once.

There are five cousins living at Dadi's house in Islamabad—all between four and eleven years of age—and their palto names, or nicknames, are:

1. Bachee—10
2. Bibi—9½
3. Bun-toe—7
4. Bun-tee—6
5. Bacha—11½

Bacha is the same age as me, but he's grown four inches since the last time I saw him! There's some dirt on his upper lip too. He's the closest person I have to a brother. But he's also the only cousin not talking to me! Whenever we visited Isloo before, Bacha and I played long, elaborate marble matches together. We found spots in every corner of my grandmother's house and shot our marbles against each other's. We were best buds, right? You would think so, but this year he doesn't even want to look at me! Why doesn't he want to play marbles anymore? What's wrong with him?

Wednesday, June 12, 1991

After dinner, I cornered Bacha as he was coming out of the washroom.

"We need to talk, Bacha." As soon as the words left my lips, he started shaking. His eyes wouldn't meet mine and his gaze darted nervously back and forth across the floor. "Why won't you play with me?" I asked.

"Let me go."

"Answer me first." I moved toward him. Did I need to twist his pinky finger?

"Okay, okay. Uncle. My father said I'm not allowed to be in a room alone with a girl."

"Huh?"

"He said if I'm in a room alone with a girl a baby will come."

I froze. A baby? I imagined a tiny brown human materializing on the floor between us. Stubby legs kicking. Fists punching the air. In my mind's eye, I saw it to begin to bawl. It's face turned red. It was tiny. Loud. Angry. More horrifying than all this, half it's face looked like mine. The other half looked like Bacha's.

"B-b-but I'm your cousin," I stammered, confused.

Bacha shuddered.

"*Any* girl."

Then he cradled his belly, raised his eyebrows and looked at me accusingly.

I saw myself scooping up the baby off the floor. With my right hand I was rubbing its back. With my other hand I was frying onions.

My face turned white.

I moved out of my cousin's way. "You'd better go. Quick."

Bacha sighed in relief and skipped out of the room.

Thursday, June 13, 1991

I've discovered that Bacha and I were silly to be so worried! It's impossible to be alone here. There are so many people in Dadi's house, and every room always has an auntie or uncle coming or leaving. Look, there is Uncle Baloo pulling a long telephone cord behind him. Unmarried. Tutoo and I call him "the Giant." Actually this is a nickname from the neighboring kids. He is six foot seven. He is at work most of the day, and the rest of the time he tries to find quiet corners from which to make crank calls to bored Isloo housewives. And there goes Uncle Gollu Mollu, or Uncle Roly-Poly. Uncle Gollu Mollu is a kind, quiet type, so we draw on his arms and steal his slippers. And do you hear that? That's Sibbi Phuppo, my father's oldest sister. She just called me from the kitchen. Some new dish is ready. She loves cooking for others (which really means she loves watching others eat), and at any given hour of any given day, the dining table is full of her homemade cooking. Halwa puri and pakoras and samosas and chana chaat and dahi baray and nan khatai and zeera biscuits are just some of the snacks that she keeps revolving on the table in between our mealtimes.

Mehman-nawazi, or being hospitable, is a very serious thing in Pakistan, and this means Tutoo and I have to try everything on the table so we don't insult anyone's cooking. We also don't need to wait to be asked three times to eat in this house because this is family, and family means you will never, ever go hungry, in a thousand different ways.

Friday, June 14, 1991

The biggest news at Dadi's house concerns Jibbi Phuppo, Aba's youngest sister. The big news is that she has no news. Which means she failed to find a husband last year.

Dadi and our aunties teased her on the first night we got here, and they haven't stopped since. "Poor Jibbi—so unlucky. Even bad-tempered-you-know-who got married last year. And that one, oh-ho, the one who can't make a proper cup of chai! Even *she* got scooped up."

Dadi has told Jibbi Phuppo, the twenty-two-year-old unmarried spinster of the family, to be in charge of feeding and bathing the seven kids now in the house for the summer: that's me, Tutoo and our five cousins who live here. Dadi also put her in charge of refereeing all our games and arguments. "That'll teach her to be picky," Dadi muttered under her breath after she had listed all of Jibbi Phuppo's chores.

After dinner, my cousin Bachee pulled me aside and whispered that Jibbi Phuppo has a handsome friend with a motorcycle who comes to visit her when Dadi's not home. And that if we don't tell on Jibbi Phuppo, then our aunt will give us little rectangles of pink bubblegum, shiny beads and buttons, *and* we might even be allowed to wipe down her handsome friend's motorcycle.

Saturday, June 15, 1991

This vacation is going to be a total drab, dreary bummer of a summer! I spent the entire day watching the ceiling fans circulate hot air. I counted eight chipkali or lizards that scurried up and down the walls. At sunset, the sky was pink and blue and the mooti, or jasmine flowers, in Dadi's back garden bloomed and burst into scent.

Oh, to be forced to spend a *whole* summer in such idle leisure!! I just know I am going to remember this as the worst summer of my life.

Why Dadi's house is no fun:
1. There is no TV. We are bored.
2. There is no AC. We are melting.
3. There is no English.

Tutoo and I are forced to use our foreign mother tongue, Urdu. Our mother tongue comes out broken and jagged, and we put the emphasis on the wrong syllables, and our cousins laugh at us.

Sunday, June 16, 1991

I suppose Isloo has one or two good things that Dubai doesn't have, and one of them is the monsoon season. In the summer months, every seven or ten days there is a massive thunderstorm where the sky opens up and there is an all-out, non-stop pelting of rain, or barsaat, that cuts the heat.

As soon as we heard the first few droplets hit the windows this morning, us kids rushed to the rooftop terrace to play in the rain. After ten minutes, the girls had to go inside as our clothes turned see-through. The boys got to stay outside for longer, as boys' clothing must not be see-through.

After the storm petered out and we changed into dry clothes, a high, thin humming sound came floating up from the street—the pungi-wallah was making his rounds! The pungi is the flute that snake charmers use, and snake charmers in Isloo are like an ice cream cart going by in Dubai. The

pungi-wallah came by with a few harmless snakes and a dancing cobra in his wicker basket. Perched on his shoulder was
a cheeky monkey. We grabbed fruit for the monkey, who
then climbed down, saluted each of us, and performed a few
magic tricks.

Feeling bonded because we had witnessed the monsoon,
dancing snakes, and magic tricks from a monkey, Tutoo and
I joined the cousins in a type of hide-and-seek game that
our cousins call "Refugee." Only one person hides (the refugee), and everyone else is a seeker. The seekers have to work
alone, and they fan out to find the refugee. The seeker who
finds the refugee first quietly becomes a refugee too and has
to hide with the refugee in the same spot, and so on and so
on until everyone is crammed into the same small space. The
last finder is the big stinky *loser* and becomes the first refugee
in the next round. Dadi's place has lots of great hiding spots
to cram into. Some of my favorites:

1. Under the big bed in the attic.
2. Behind the flower bushes in Dadi's back garden.
3. Up in the branches of the banyan tree in the
   front garden.
4. Stuffed into the closet in Dadi's room.

The problem with this last spot was that we had to re-
arrange all of Dadi's shalwar kameez and saris and jewelry
boxes to fit ourselves inside the shelves properly, and Dadi's

blood pressure shot sky-high when she saw that we didn't put things back neatly.

As punishment, none of us were given any mango seeds to suck on at dinnertime. It was still worth it, as it was such a fun time playing with our cousins, and as a bonus, the longer we played, the faster and correct-er our Urdu came out—though maybe now we are un-remembering our English. It's a small price to pay because these games have so much fun-ness! I just know that this is going to be the bestest summer ever!

Monday, June 17, 1991

At breakfast, Dadi told us that she was going to spend the day at the chai-wallah's shop, and that we were not allowed to play any games that would have us tearing through the house making a mess like jungli, or wild animals, so Jibbi Phuppo dusted off our late Dada's wooden chessboard and took us to the attic. We older cousins explained the rules to the younger ones.

We were supposed to stay in the attic quietly all afternoon, taking turns playing chess, but it didn't work out that way. Bun-toe and Bun-tee, the littlest ones at six and seven, kept forgetting the rules. Bachee and Bibi cried every time they lost a piece, even the unimportant ones. Tutoo kept cheating by moving the pieces when she thought no one was looking. And Bacha was shockingly better at chess than I was! The pandemonium.

We made a loud racket after each game, tearfully accusing each other of cheating. Some of the sore losers even pinched and pulled the winners' hair (mostly Bun-toe and Bun-tee and okay, I did it a few times too).

Ami complained about her growing bump, faked a headache and stayed locked-up in her room all day reading naughty books.

Bun-toe and Bun-tee were put to bed early. After their bedtime, Tutoo tried to impress the older cousins with stories about her toys in Dubai. A remote-control car with windows that go up and down. A teddy bear as big as an actual bear. Dollhouses with working light bulbs. Then she told them that every room in every home in Dubai has an AC that stays on all day, every day. Bachee rolled her eyes, and Bibi and Bacha guffawed, pointing their palms in Tutoo's face, taunting her with the nickname they've given her—"Sheikha," the Arabic word for queen.

Tuesday, June 18, 1991

The grown-ups sat in Dadi's living room discussing the headlines in this week's newspapers—"Breaking: Refugee Influx Fans Religious Divisions" and "Breaking: Pakistan's President Promises New Sharia Laws to Appease Mullahs" and "Breaking: Unemployment in Pakistan Reaches Record Levels—*Again*."

The grown-ups blamed the headlines on Pakistan's "mullah mafia"—powerful religious groups that hurt the daily lives of ordinary Pakistanis. The mullahs are why my Dadi can't find fresh vegetables. Why my cousins don't know when the electricity will go out and for how long. Why no one knows when a newspaper might shut down, when journalists might be arrested and how then to get information about the weather or road closures or job openings.

Our older uncles lamented that the mullah mafia was born out of the ten-year Soviet-Afghanistan war that started in 1979 and only wrapped up two years ago. During that time, millions of Afghan refugees poured into Pakistan. The American forces stood behind the Afghan forces, plying them with guns and bullets and dollar bills, and in turn, who else but the yuck-o Saudi forces stood behind the American ones. The grown-ups argued about who was worse, the Americans or the Saudis? And they complained that Pakistanis in positions of power weren't much better—even though Pakistan had elected a woman prime minister last year, there still hadn't been any change in the rights and lives of women. *Corruption*, *nepotism* and *cronyism* were other words the grown-ups railed against. In the end, the only thing everyone agreed on was that politics in our part of the world was a dizzying madhouse of mirrors and, as usual, it was us ordinary people who were forced to endure blackouts, wilted vegetables and censored movies.

In the evening, Bachee and Bacha took Tutoo and me to see the mosque down the street. They pointed to their favorite spot behind the raat ki rani shrubs, from where they throw tomatoes at the one-legged imam who leads the prayers inside. They said they are sure the One-legged Imam is a mullah in disguise and therefore our sworn enemy. When he emerged from the mosque after prayers, his beady eyes and beard *did* look positively villainous, so we pelted him with tomatoes and ran for our lives.

On the run back home from the mosque, a crow followed us, screeching, "Allah, Allah!" We cried hot tears of fear all the way home. Once we crossed the gates into our courtyard, we fell on our hands and knees laughing.

Wednesday, June 19, 1991

Tutoo's stories of the Great-Expat-Dubai-Life are getting more and more outrageous. She loves our cousins, but she also loves to remind them that we are the "Dubai cousins" and are therefore richer and smarter and better than they are. I'm not sure where she learnt all this snobbery!

Before breakfast, Tutoo told the cousins that there were more sweets on the dining table at her birthday party this year than all the sweets at the mithai-wallah's shop down the road. After breakfast, she told them there are moving staircases in Dubai that take you all the way up to Heaven, that she's been there and that Heaven is dizzying and magical, like a mouthful of ice cubes, not softening and smelly, like melting guavas in summertime Isloo.

In the afternoon, Bibi moved calmly toward Tutoo and, in one quick movement, bit her cheek, drawing blood. Tutoo shrieked so loudly that the neighbors came running over. There was blood running down Tutoo's shirt. Jibbi Phuppo told the neighbors, "Dubai cousins se jealousy," and they all nodded and went back home.

Afterwards, we tried to play games with our cousins, but there was more pushing and pinching and name-calling. After the biting, it feels like a line has been drawn between us—the Isloo cousins and the Dubai cousins.

After Bibi bit Tutoo, I waited until Bibi was alone in the back garden, held her down and made both her arms red with pinch marks until she promised to never bite Tutoo again. You see, it's not at all Tutoo's fault that she brags about our Dubai life! Tutoo is just a huge copycat and must be copying someone. ~~Me~~. Besides, how can Tutoo and I be expected to get along with our cousins if Tutoo and I live such better lives than them?

Bibi went crying to Jibbi Phuppo and told on me for pinching her. Then Bibi spent the rest of the evening showing off the red pinch marks to all the aunts and uncles, as if they were badges of honor. "See, I told you, didn't I, that anyone who grows up in Dubai becomes a meanie! A snob! A heartless boo-boo-booger," she wailed all night. Before bedtime, Jibbi Phuppo lined up all the girl cousins in the washroom. She spread soap in rough strokes, then dumped buckets of cold water over our stinging eyes and shivering bodies, one by one.

"Not one of you is better than any other," she said, making sure to look at none of us.

Thursday, June 20, 1991

Jibbi Phuppo woke all of us early and marched us up the dark stairway to the roof. The door swung open. Hot white light flooded our eyes, then slowly faded into color. Rainbow wings shimmered all around us. We had walked into a swarm of dragonflies. Jibbi Phuppo plucked one from the air, looped a piece of string around its body, and bit the string off with her teeth. She handed each of us an insect-kite, one at a time.

The winged creatures flew in circles around our heads for two minutes or twenty minutes or maybe two hundred years. "Look. Listen," Jibbi Phuppo said. "There are joys in nature and in our hearts that all the money in Dubai cannot buy. Remember that not one of you is better than the other, so give to and take from each other freely."

The colors were so beautiful and the creatures so magical that Jibbi Phuppo's words played in a loop in my head all day.

After hours of cooking and cleaning, I watched Dadi sit down with two needles and a ball of wool, like she does every night. She pulled and looped the rough wool to create a shape and warmth for Bibi. A bright-red wool sweater with mother-of-pearl buttons. *There are joys in nature and in our hearts that all the money in Dubai cannot buy.* The Isloo cousins have closets full of handmade sweaters that Dadi's gnarled, shaky hands make with love each year, and that get passed down with pride. I thought of my closets in Dubai that are bulging with brand-new clothes for Tutoo and me, some with their price tags still on, and it made me wonder.

Friday, June 21, 1991

The grown-ups have decided to let us cousins play *outside* the house. They believe allowing us to spend the day outside together will achieve two important goals:

1. Unite us as a team; and
2. Keep the house quiet and peaceful for themselves.

The two rules are that we must stay in a group the whole time and that the one kid bike in the house must be shared between the seven of us. Bachee and I share the saddle, but she does the pedaling and leans right. Tutoo sits on the handlebar at the front, and she and I lean left. Bibi and Bun-tee fit themselves into the basket at the back, their knees at their ears. Bacha and Bun-toe run alongside the bike. Isloo is such a friendly city that on every bike ride, people laugh and give us thumbs-ups! In Dubai we would get finger wagging and tickets.

As long as we stay in a group and come back before sunset, we are allowed to go as far down as the mosque with the One-legged Imam and as far up as the forest, where the leaves are so big and thick that people cut them off and hold them over their heads as umbrellas.

Saturday, June 22, 1991

We went to the hill where we found a dead baby bird last week and Bachee showed us a game called Seven Stones. The game was a bit like dodgeball and cricket jumbled up together!

We were having so much fun that we didn't notice how late it had gotten until we heard the One-legged Imam's call for Maghrib prayers, and then we looked up and saw bright stars poking through the soft purple sky. We raced down the hill all the way home like wolves were at our heels!

Who knew that games played outside could be so much fun—I hardly felt the insects, the dust or the heat!

Sunday, June 23, 1991

Eid ul Adha today. The grown-ups made all the preparations and us kids just needed to show up and stay out of the way.

This Eid is the Big One. It's also known as Bakra Eid (Goat Eid), or Bari Eid (Big Eid), or Qurbani Eid (Sacrifice Eid). I could also call it Khooni Eid (Bloody Eid) because of all the blood. There were red rivers running down Isloo's streets, and the wailing and bleating by goats and cows and sheep was so loud that I had to cup my ears.

After witnessing all that horror, I gorged myself on mutton biryani and mutton paya and mutton liver and Bihari kebab and shami kebab and chapli kebab and galouti kebab and went back for seconds and thirds. Now that I've eaten as much meat as I could in twenty-four hours, I've decided to become vegetarian. (Until next year's Bakra Eid, that is.)

Monday, June 24, 1991

We spent the day playing Kho-Kho on the roof. This game is a bit like playing tag but there are two teams, and one team has to line up in a row and stay there, and the chaser has to capture someone strategically and not just willy-nilly run after them, and you can tap someone in the row to become the chaser instead and . . . well, okay, so maybe it's not at all like tag. The kids in Isloo play such different games from the kids in Dubai!

Isn't it so strange that kids all around the world play different kinds of games but have the exact same amount of fun?

Tuesday, June 25, 1991

After spending our days outside, we come back to Dadi's house looking like little jinns, or ghouls. Small bits of flowers and leaves and twigs in our hair. Muddy knees. Earth packed deeply under our nails. Our eyes wild with glee. Jibbi Phuppo takes us into the washroom every evening and as she pours buckets of warm water over our heads, we share the day's adventures and exploits with her. She is the only grown-up who listens to our stories with interest and patience. Our parents have completely disappeared, and I'd forgotten how nice it is to come to Pakistan and be spoiled by the attention from our extended family and get a break from our parents! Ami's been so happy to see us having fun with our cousins that she hasn't seemed to mind one bit that the color on our faces and arms has deepened to a sun-kissed brown.

"Aur sunao!"—And let's hear more!—Jibbi Phuppo always implores.

We tell her about the loveliness of ladybugs that flew into Bun-toe's palm the other day, or the blossom drop of orange-tipped white shafali flowers that carpeted Next-Door Uncle's garden last week. The other grown-ups just want talk to about politics and the headlines with each other. They're always grumbling about the mullahs and the damage they are doing to Pakistan. Pakistan's mullah mafia is all that concerns them! Who cares about those things! Either they've forgotten or they ignore the important things in life:

1. Slurping on mango seeds after dinner.
2. Linking arms with your cousins and skipping downhill.
3. Sleeping on the rooftop under a sky brimful of stars.

Wednesday, June 26, 1991

At the sweetshop today, the mithai wallah, or sweets seller, narrowed his eyes at me and said, "You don't look Pakistani. You look Indian. Where are you from?" I shrugged and told him I'm a muhajir.

Bachee, standing next to me, pinched my arm and hissed in my ear, "Uffo, *you* can't call yourself muhajir! That's a dirty word others use for us."

Pakistanis call us muhajirs because my father's family are the Muslims that came to Pakistan from elsewhere. It's not as bad as being an Afghan refugee, but it's not as good as being a pakka, or pure Pakistani, either.

Because we are muhajirs, there is nothing in Dadi's house that is older than twenty years. No jewelry, no photo, no book. No story is told that goes back before those twenty years. Every memory they talk to us about comes after that long night when Aba's family walked under the stars from Dhaka in Bangladesh to Islamabad in Pakistan during the Pakistan-Bangladesh war of 1971. They left their homes and bank accounts, favorite trees and gravestones in the middle of the night and walked under the stars for about a week or so. What happened during that walk, and their lives before that walk, is something the grown-ups refuse to talk to us about.

Friday, June 28, 1991

Our uncles borrowed Next-Door Uncle's minivan and we all went to Margalla Hills. We turned the radio up full-blast and sang along at the top of our lungs to "Dil, Dil Pakistan," which is only the world's most famous song, sung by the world's most famous band, Vital Signs. Vital Signs are four boys from Isloo's neighboring city, Pindi, who formed a pop band in college. Next up, the radio played Vital Signs' newest song, which came piping hot out of the record studio this month! It's called "Sanwali Saloni" and is much slower but super catchy. It's already become this summer's biggest hit— it's about a dusky-skinned beauty whose shiny bangles make all the boys swoon!

I guess this explains why my mother isn't bothered by our tans anymore—she finally realizes she was wrong about what it takes to be one of the pretty girls!! No more skin-lightening paste from now on. We just need to find shiny bangles instead.

The ride in the minivan was so bumpy that Bun-tee threw up three times! And Bun-toe needed four pee-stops! During each vomit and bladder pit stop, Bacha caught my eye and smirked smugly. His look told me what he was thinking—*See, I'm not going to make a dum-dum mistake and end up like these fathers! No one's going to catch me in a room alone with a girl.*

We had a great day walking around town, and we stopped for a picnic at a park. *Well*, it was great until three big boys jogged behind Jibbi Phuppo and started shouting bad things and singing songs. Four other big boys laughed by the side of the road.

When bad men bother girls on TV, there are always handsome heroes to the rescue. I kept my eyes peeled but no such luck!

The only ones who came running to protect Jibbi Phuppo were her own brothers—our uncles. *YUCK!* Given their aching backs and potbellies, it wasn't the kind of thing a young girl should ever have to see. Our uncles can't even bring down a mosquito without pulling a muscle! Their only weapons of attack were loud voices and balding heads.

Saturday, June 29, 1991

A letter arrived from Laila today! The tissue-thin cotton paper was damp from the humidity. It read—

Dearest Mona,

School closed for summer break yesterday! My mother's put me in swimming lessons and piano lessons for the next two months. Worse than this, she is making me babysit my brothers every Thursday evening because she's put herself in belly-dancing lessons.

Worser than all this combined, I heard through Sobia's brother's cousin's friend that Waleed sent an origami swan to Maryam. I did my best friend duty and told Maryam, "You can't reply! He's Mona's One True Love," but Maryam said (and I quote her true and exact words): "Mona is moving away to the Land of Igloos, so why not? Besides, I'm excellent at sharing, and Mona and I can both share, just like Muhammed's wives."

How is your summer going?

Love,

Laila

!!!!!

Oh Life, how doth thine blade twist and turn and plunge itself deep into the deepest depths of my deep, deep soul!

Eulogy for Waleed by Mona Hasan, 11½
To the louse named Waleed,
You did an unforgiveable deed.

Soon in Canada I shall be
Where think of thee

135

I shall not.
In Dubai you will always be hot
and rot.

'Tis a shame our love was lost in thy greed,
Fare thee well, lousy louse Waleed!

This poem might need some tweaking, but it's off to a very good start, if I must say so myself.

Sunday, June 30, 1991

Aba once told me that the hardest thing in life is to love someone. Today I am wiser than my father because I have learned that the truth is that there is something harder still—not to love someone.

CHAPTER SEVEN

July

Monday, July 1, 1991

Waleed—a thousand years have passed since I last saw you but I'm still stuck in that space where our eyes met.

Tuesday, July 2, 1991

I spent the whole day in the dusty attic, crying aloud to sad love songs on the radio. How could I be so cruelly betrayed by my One True Love?

As if she somehow sensed that I needed her, a letter from Hala arrived for me today—

Dear Mona,

Do you have any poetry books at your grandmother's? During times of sorrow, poetry fills the fault lines.

Do you know of Khalil Gibran? He has a poem that is a balm during times of upheaval called "On Joy and Sorrow." He says that the clay pot that holds our honey is the same pot that is burned in a potter's oven. That flutes that play the music that soothes our spirits are made of the same wood that are first carved by knives. He promises that the deeper the sorrow that hollows out our soul, the deeper the joy that will one day satiate it.

Will you believe that deep pain and difficulty arrive only to make us better, not bitter?

Love, Hala

Wednesday, July 3, 1991

I suppose what Hala is trying to tell me is that great poets believe that deep suffering will one day bring great joy, like the clay cup after it's been through fire. Or the flute that's been cut by a knife.

The only thing that is clear to me is that reading all that Russian literature has done something to Hala's brain!

Ya Allah, please limit my life to one of mediocre difficulty and mediocre joy.

The Clay Pot by Mona Hasan, 11½
I do not
Even one jot
want to be a hot
fraught
clay pot.

I used the fancy paper hidden in Dadi's closet to write a short reply to Hala. I also put in some of my favorite pressed petals—

Dear Hala,
There are zero books of poetry at my Dadi's.
I did find Khalil Gibran's book of poetry at Next-Door Uncle's. Next-Door Uncle is the only one on this block who has a minivan and a shelf full of poetry books. But I'm not sure Gibran is such a good poet. I mean, none of his poems even rhyme! How embarrassing!!
Love, Mona

Thursday, July 4, 1991

Listening to all these love songs over and over has made one thing crystal clear—love STINKS! I am never falling in love again!

I was ready to emerge from the attic anyway, but Bachee came to coax me out by walking in with a cane basket full of juicy, ripe tomatoes. She stood by the window where the light streams in so it looked like the tomatoes were on fire. She smiled, then winked. "Chalo. Our day awaits," she beckoned and pulled me into the heat.

Friday, July 5, 1991

The One-legged Imam dropped by after jummah prayers. He told Dadi he has no proof that we are the tomato throwers, but he has no proof that we are *not* the tomato throwers either. He lifted his shalwar and showed us his wooden leg. Even though we were allowed to touch it, none of us wanted to.

In case we were the tomato throwers, Dadi and Jibbi Phuppo made us bow down our heads and say sorry to him. In case we weren't, we had to swear to defend him against the tomato-throwing gang of hooligans. We tugged at the skin on our throats and shouted, "Allahu Akbar," and swore to defend him against the raised-in-a-zoo hooligans attacking a man of God. Then Dadi and Jibbi Phuppo fed him all our best pieces of lamb.

He studied the dent on Tutoo's left arm from her polio shot for a long time, then limped home. Later in the evening, he rang the bell at the gate, smiled at us with his crooked teeth and limped off to the neighbor's house. By our gate, he had propped up a cricket bat and four tennis balls wrapped in black electrical tape.

Saturday, July 6, 1991

We went to the hill where we found the dead baby bird and made a wicket with twigs and sticks and split into two teams.

I wanted to be the batsman today. The ball was sometimes Maryam's little heart and sometimes Waleed's itty-bitty four-chambered organ. Each time the ball was lobbed toward me, I managed to smash the blood and guts out of it. Watching the ball soar past my cousins, past the neighborhood kids, past branches, past leaves helped me turn the pain into anger. Batting felt like loosening a tap to let out a rush of water.

Playing these games with my cousins this summer has taught me that I've been wasting my time focusing on the unremarkable things—how big my gazoongas get and what my body *looks* like is not anywhere as astonishing and incredible as what my body can *do*.

Sunday, July 7, 1991

Yesterday we lost all four of our cricket balls in the dense bushes and shrubs. So today we made Bun-tee climb guava trees and pluck the smallest, greenest guavas off branches. We used the guavas as cricket balls. The hard, unripe guavas worked just as well as the cricket balls.

Today I was a fielder, and I realized that fielding is just as important a position as batting, maybe even more so.

It's in the many moments of waiting for my chance to get at the ball that I have to remember to breathe slowly, watch the ball and be patient. I have to remember that my chance may be coming up, even if it feels like I've been waiting forever. I have to remind myself that I can yet make a difference in the game if I pay attention and look for my opening. I just have to remember to not get distracted, to not feel defeated and to keep giving it my all. The best games are the ones where I'm putting everything in and my back gets slick with sweat and there's a sheen of wetness on my face and my heart is beating to jump out of its cage. And if I still fail—face-first on the ground, dirt in my mouth, blood on my elbows and knees—then I still get back up in the game and give it my all. I must remember that I only ever lose if I stop playing.

Cricket by Mona Hasan, 11½
Cricket soothes my soul
Whether I bat, field or bowl
Cricket fills the angry hole.

Monday, July 8, 1991

The cousins, Tutoo and I found fifteen caterpillar cocoons today! The cocoons were silky green cases hanging off bushes, and we plucked them carefully and divided them equally among us. We're storing them inside our uncles' empty cigarette boxes for now. We decorated the cigarette boxes with our names and drawings, then we wet the boxes and hung the cocoons upside down by the windowsill, like Jibbi Phuppo showed us. With a little sunlight and some water, we'll see new winged creatures emerge from our boxes in a few weeks.

Tuesday, July 9, 1991

Before breakfast, the One-legged Imam stopped by to drop off two music cassettes that he'd received for free with his toothpaste. He said with a sheepish smile, "I thought the children might enjoy." I watched as his eyes lingered on Jibbi Phuppo's face.

Daft old man! At his age, it's dead shameful that he hasn't yet realized that Love is a one-way road to misery. Last week, Jibbi Phuppo told us cousins that she's in love with Motorcycle-Wallah and is ready to tell Dadi as soon as the timing is opportune. Foolish old people!

Wednesday, July 10, 1991

This morning, I saw red on the bedsheets and on my legs and thought death was coming for me. Dadi was the first grown-up I saw when I peeked my head out of the bedroom so I wailed out, "My beloved Dadi, come quick! I am at death's door." Dadi slipped inside, shook me and calmed me down. Then she gave me a box of Kotex and told me I was having my big-girl time of the month. "Calm yourself. It's just blood between your legs. You won't die." Easy for her to say! She's a hundred years old and death has still not come for her!

Dadi and I spent the afternoon soaking and washing the sheets. She showed me how to make a paste out of baking soda and lemon, and we blotted and wrung the sheets to erase any trace of red. Then up on the roof, we hung the wet sheets to dry in the white afternoon light. As we waited, Dadi told me, "Sports are for younger girls, Mona. Take a break for a while. The blood might leak. Stain your clothes."

Ya Allah, I couldn't play sports even if I wanted to! I can barely walk with this cotton brick in my underwear.

Thursday, July 11, 1991

How have we put a person on the moon but we haven't yet found a comfortable solution for the big-girl time of the month? We need machines to make the right kind of menstrual underwear for every girl in every country! We also need machines to clean all the stains! I can't be expected to do this kind of laundry once a month for the rest of my life! In the movie *Aliens*, Ripley could *only* have beaten up the bad aliens in outer space. On earth, she'd be too busy scrubbing period stains with an old toothbrush.

Friday, July 12, 1991

Of course, I did already know all about periods because I'm the smartest girl I know, and I understand all these things inside out. Everyone told me it was going to happen, so I absolutely, definitely knew it was going to happen. But no one told me *when* the blood was going to come and *how* it was going to feel, so actually it was a bloody shock on multiple levels.

What I still don't understand is how my pee and the blood comes out of the same hole . . . or are there two different holes?? Bodies are so gross, but also so fascinating. Miracles of strength and creation, I guess. Mrs. Adila has never discussed the female body at school. "It's not in our textbooks, girls. You'll learn all about the female body when you get into doctor school," she sometimes says. "Or when you have your first child," she sometimes mutters.

> **The Hole by Mona Hasan, 11½**
> My school tried to control
> What I could know about my hole
> Not knowing took a toll
> On the soul.

Saturday, July 13, 1991

After breakfast, I told my Dadi I had some questions about the blood pouring out of me every month. I could have asked my mother, but Dadi's in charge of everything around here, so I thought it was wisest to ask her. I asked her my burning questions: *Why does blood have to come out of my yooha at all? How long is this going to continue? How have we built machines to put a man on the moon but not created machines to help women with the leaks?*

Dadi studied me carefully. "The day has come to teach you some big-girl things." She took me aside and told me that the blood that came pouring out of me every month was a blessing and a signal that I had become a woman, and that now that I was a woman, I could fulfill my purpose in life— marriage! She leaned in and whispered that with Allah's help and a pious grandmother's prayers, I would receive many rishtas—marriage proposals—to help me in my goal.

She told me that in order to get the most number of rishtas, I must never, ever forget the number-one rule of being a marriageable woman—modesty.

Modesty had everything to do with the type of clothes I wore, she said. She reminded me that no girls during the time of the Venerable Hazrat Muhammad (may peace be upon Him) wore today's immodest clothing—the scandalous T-shirt and pants.

"Chee chee, Mona—do you really want to be a T-shirt type of girl?"

How could I tell my beloved Dadi that I had a closet full of T-shirts in Dubai? And that most were short-sleeved!!! Dadi seemed to be the full-sleeves type.

"What about pants, Dadi? My entire leg is covered if I wear pants. That should be okay, right?"

Dadi put her hand up to her forehead. She was getting faint at the very thought of me in pants.

Dadi told me that if I was a modest woman, then only would the right rishtas come, but that even if that didn't work and I didn't get a doctor or engineer for a husband, then Allah could yet bless my marriage with sons. "Let your husband and sons wear the T-shirts and pants." Dadi sniffed. Why would I want to be *like* a man when I could be the *wife* of a man? The *mother* of some?

Red by Mona Hasan, 11½
So much depends
upon reds
on beds.

Sunday, July 14, 1991

Not only is blood *still* spurting out of my nether regions, but Ami has just told us that we are going to visit our Nanijaan and Nanajaan, her parents, and spend a week with them.

Isloo is arranged in a grid, and they live in the fancy part of it, which is far away, so we are leaving bright and early tomorrow morning. Tutoo and I packed small carry-on bags. I'm nervous for two big reasons. One, I have to dispose of my bloody cotton pads properly at Nanijaan's because even though my blessing and signal has arrived, it seems that I must always hide from the world that this is so. While it's okay to see blood from monsters and wars on TV, blood from my yooha is just too filthy for anyone to be subjected to. The second reason is that there are no cousins at Nanijaan and Nanajaan's, and I'm not sure how Tutoo and I will pass the time. Tutoo and I don't know our grandparents on our mother's side very well at all.

Ami doesn't say much about her parents except that they have very set ideas about what is "proper." Aba doesn't say much about them either. Whenever the topic of my mother's parents comes up, Aba pulls the newspaper in front of his face. Aba has decided not to come on our week-long visit today because Next-Door Uncle needs help with his minivan, and it might take a few days to sort it out. How a banker knows anything useful about fixing cars is a mystery to all of us!

Monday, July 15, 1991

Nanijaan gasped when she greeted the three of us at the front door. "Are you letting them out during the afternoon sun?" she asked my mother reproachfully. Ami smiled. She has been humming the song about the dusky-skinned beauty from the radio too. Nanijaan frowned. Then sighed. Limply extended her arms for Tutoo and myself to walk into obediently.

Nanajaan and Nanijaan's house is the same as I remembered from three years ago. White rugs and shiny crystal doodads behind glass cabinets. Three years ago, I put a whoopee cushion on Nanijaan's favorite armchair. That's when I found out that Nanijaan doesn't like farting games, raucous laughter or girls with too "big-big" eyes. This visit she's making Tutoo and me sit in her living room with our hands under us. We are allowed to watch melodramatic PTV dramas with her, but only if we stay quiet and don't interrupt with questions. If we are still bored, we can go count (but not touch) the books in her library, or polish (but not pocket) the silverware in her cabinet, or walk (but not run) in her garden (and only when the sun has gone down).

Tuesday, July 16, 1991

There is no kulfi, or ice cream, after dinner at Nanijaan's and Nanajaan's. They are the type of grandparents who eat dinner with forks and knives.

Tutoo thinks that they have pinched faces because they never got over the British leaving India. I think she heard Aba say this once. In any case, this theory actually makes a lot of sense. It also explains why they eat yuck-o marmite sandwiches with their chai.

Wednesday, July 17, 1991

This morning, Nanajaan kept himself hidden behind two Pakistani newspapers. He first read *The Daily Jang*, an Urdu newspaper, then he read *Dawn*, the English newspaper, to double-check the facts, or was it the other way around? He read silently and didn't tell Tutoo or me any funny stories. Aba always finds a funny story in the newspaper to share with Tutoo and me. He likes to say, "Lots of silliness in newspapers if you are reading correctly."

I can see now why Ami made her own marriage. *There are joys in nature and in our hearts that all the money in all the world cannot buy.*

Thursday, July 18, 1991

There are 126 books in Nanijaan and Nanajaan's library. But I'm taking a wild guess that there is nothing about tongue-kissing in these books.

Friday, July 19, 1991

I guess I've been wrong all this time and someone is not actually rich when they can buy things easily. The truth is that people are only ever rich when they can give and take love freely.

Saturday, July 20, 1991

I never know what to say to Nanijaan. I want to say something witty and brilliant and make her laugh. But I end up giving timid one-word answers to her clipped questions instead.

"How is school?"

"Good."

"Are you getting good marks?"

"Yes."

"Are you reading the Quran every day?"

"Yes?"

"What about Kipling?"

"Yes. Her too."

I don't think Ami knows what to say to Nanijaan either:

"When is the baby due?"

"December."

"Do you know if it's a boy or a girl?"

". . ."

"Don't you want to know?"

"Does it matter?"

". . ."

Sunday, July 21, 1991

CAPITAL *F* FREEDOM! We are going back to Dadi's tomorrow!

Monday July 22, 1991

During our final breakfast together, Nanijaan and Nanajaan gave their opinions about our move to Canada. Nanajaan told stories about the friends of friends who have gone to Canada and suffered terribly. He gave us reports about doctors driving cabs, dentists bagging groceries and bankers cleaning toilets.

As we were leaving, Nanijaan grabbed Tutoo and me, recited Ayatul Qursi, patted down our hair, then blew on our faces to ward off the evil eye. On the ride home, Tutoo complained that Nanijaan got spit in her eye, and asked what good was getting rid of the evil eye if your own grandmother's spit was in your eye instead.

Tuesday, July 23, 1991

Tutoo and I missed our cousins terribly! But it appears that they were too busy to miss us back!

There's a kite-flying festival called Basant that happens every year in Pakistan. Tutoo and I always miss it because it happens in springtime and we only visit during summertime.

However, while we were gone, Next-Door Uncle bought brand-new kites for all the kids on the street. In Pakistan, when something good happens to you, like Next-Door Uncle's minivan working again, you have to spread the goodness and do something tip-top for someone else, which is why Next-Door Uncle was harangued to buy all the kids on his street brand-new kites! That's the good news.

The bad news is that since we were away, our cousins got first dibs on the biggest, brightest kites.

Tutoo and I spent the day on the rooftop trying to bring down our cousins' kites by cutting their kite strings with our own kite strings. Unfortunately, our cousins are expert kite flyers, so we weren't able to bring theirs down, but at least they were kind enough not to cut ours. When the wind picked up our kites and danced them high, it felt like it wasn't just our kites that were wild and free in the sky. It felt like we were soaring right alongside, too.

Thursday, July 25, 1991

Jibbi Phuppo didn't get to finish our bedtime story tonight because motorcycle-wallah came to take her for a ride down the street. "Oh-ho! What a hero!" our other aunties teased as she left through the back door. Jibbi Phuppo's cheeks flashed red, but her eyes were smiling and she held her head high. Now we have to wait until tomorrow night to find out the ending to her story!

Since he interrupted our storytime, we have decided that we are not going to wash motorcycle-wallah's bike next time he visits, and Tutoo has promised to stick her tongue out at him when no one is looking.

Friday, July 26, 1991

After dinnertime, Dadi made a hook with her right finger, tilted her head toward the hallway and asked Aba to follow her into the stairway. Through my super-duper eavesdropping skills, I heard Dadi complain to Aba: "a widow gets no respect from her children. You deal with Jibbi. Tell her to stay within her borders. The neighbors are talking."

Saturday, July 27, 1991

It was the most ordinary of days today but somehow Aba found the perfect moment—one he had been waiting for all along—to tell his mother that we were moving to Canada.

After we had finished our meal and everyone was setting up checkers and the carrom board, Jibbo Phuppo brought out Gibran's book of poetry. She cleared her throat and pretended to open it to a random poem. She read it out loud, translating in Urdu as she went along for Dadi—

> *Your children are not your children.*
> *They are the sons and daughters of Life's longing*
> *   for itself.*

Before she could lose courage, Jibbo Phuppo opened the floodgates. She babbled that she had invited motorcycle-wallah to send a rishta for her, which was going to be brought over tomorrow by his two aunts as his own parents had passed away when he was quite young, and would we please not judge them too harshly for lack of manners or education, and that they were fine people with love and loyalty to give if not a grand trousseau or jewelry, and could they please get married in a simple ceremony this week as the timing was of some delicate consequence, and that One-legged Imam had already been informed and had consented to help out with the hush-hush nikah ceremony. Before Dadi could have her heart attack, Jibbi Phuppo nudged Aba, who jumped in with his news next.

"My beloved mother, you must understand that everyone living in the Gulf at my salary level applied for immigration this year to the countries they are most unlikely to bomb next. We filled out the paperwork to move to Canada a while ago, and it's moving along rather quickly." He continued, "We did not want to go, but we cannot be sitting ducks either."

Everyone waited for Dadi to inhale. Or exhale. Or blink. Finally she tilted her head toward Uncle Gollu Mollu and said, in a voice shaky with false bravado, "Jildi, he must be closing up by now. Get ten boxes of laddoos. Quick."

Then Dadi hugged my parents tightly and with eyes shiny with sadness and a voice hoarse with tears, she told them, "Go. You have always had my blessing to explore this big, crazy world. It will be full of the best wonders for your children and their children that I cannot even begin to imagine, inshaAllah."

The grown-ups talked and laughed and cried into the night, and Tutoo and I fell asleep holding our cousins' hands tightly. We promised to send them stickers and stamps and posters and cassettes and diamonds and ACs from our new home in Canada.

Sunday, July 28, 1991

Shaadi business is a serious thing in Pakistan. Dadi wasn't going to let Jibbi Phuppo take away her shopping fun.

We went to Laal Kurti, or the fabric district, and walked around for days and days. Yards and yards of fabric were unrolled for us. The shopkeepers flung silks, chiffons, velvets and lace into a mountain for us. Then we walked to a different store, and Dadi swore and cursed that the prices were lower at the first one, and she repeated this over and over until someone too tired to argue gave Dadi a good deal. Afterwards we visited the tailor district, where the tailors were cajoled over compliments and chai to sew us brand-new clothes by tomorrow morning.

Monday, July 29, 1991

The next morning Dadi came to me carrying a stack of shalwar kameez that she had had made especially for me and Tutoo. I showed her the cocoons hanging by the windowsill.

They are almost ready to hatch! She sat silently and admired them with me for a bit. Then she began:

"Suno, Mona, I know I've had a lot to say to you about the clothes on your body. And maybe you're right. Maybe it's completely your business and not an iota of my business. But hear this old woman out. The British took a lot from us but not everything. We're the only people left who still wear their traditional clothing to weddings, to grocery stores, to schools. We wear it to work in, cook in, sleep in, take walks in. Sure, you're moving to a New Land and you're going to want to test out new looks and experiment, and you do that, and you barrel into your future. But remember to dip here and there into your past too. Your clothes will connect you to your culture, your history and to *me*. Remember, home is not somewhere your feet are. It's where your heart is, and some days your heart may just want to think of me. So take these clothes with you and keep them in a corner of your closet. Whenever you miss me, pull them out, dust them off and for the love of Allah, remember your Dadi with love and a little prayer."

Tuesday, July 30, 1991

To wed Jibbi Phuppo and Motorcycle Uncle, the One-legged Imam came hobbling over for the nikah ceremony. All of us girls were in our shiniest, brightest fabric, with henna on our palms, and sleeves of shiny bangles up our arms. Jibbi

Phuppo wore a fragrant necklace made of red and white marigolds, and we all agreed that there had never been a more beautiful bride. To be surrounded by flowers and your family! I think I would like a wedding day just like this, Allah.

Breathless and sweaty, One-legged Imam performed his imam duties very properly, very seriously and with only the barest hint of a broken heart.

Later Aba greened his palms very generously with Dubai dirhams.

Wednesday, July 31, 1991

A butterfly emerged from its cocoon today. There was so much wriggling and wriggling. And for so long. Why? The caterpillar was happy in its own chrysalis. It lived in there. Ate in there. It knew it was alive inside, even if it was a cramped and tight life. Why was it struggling so hard to leave? How did it have faith that the world outside wasn't full of birds and frogs and other monsters? Or did it know and it risked anyway? Oh Allah, how did it so boldly believe in the beauty of a new world?

CHAPTER EIGHT

August

Thursday, August 1, 1991

Aba's mother, Dadi, has only ever been on an airplane once in her life. After Dada, our grandfather, passed away, Aba bought Dadi a plane ticket to visit us in Dubai. This was a long time ago. Tutoo wasn't born yet, and I was only two years old.

For Dadi, stepping into Dubai was like a stepping onto another planet. She had never seen sports cars or skyscrapers. Supermarkets with overflowing produce or streetlights that always stayed lit.

On her first day in the UAE, my parents took Dadi to Al Ghurair Centre, Dubai's glitziest mall. The floors were made of marble, the lights were shining brightly and the twenty-four karat jewelry stores were lined up one after another. Dadi took one step on an escalator going down and was so stunned that she sat down on the moving step until it reached ground level. At the bottom, Aba hoisted her trembling body back up to standing and everyone around them clapped.

Friday, August 2, 1991

Aba and Ami went for the immigration interview at the Canadian embassy this morning. Since Tutoo and I are under eighteen, we didn't need to attend.

When they came back from the embassy, they told us that the immigration people asked them many questions. One of the questions was whether Aba and Ami speak any English. Aba said that they must have forgotten the British were in our countries for two hundred years.

Saturday, August 3, 1991

To prepare for our new life in North America, Tutoo and I spent the day asking everyone around us about the things they know about life in North America. Here are some of the things we learned:

Jibbi Phuppo told us that when Canadians ask, "What's up?" you are not supposed to look up. They just mean "how are you doing."

Bachee told us that *cool* is an important word at school.

You definitely don't want to be hot and sweaty; you want to be relaxed and *COOL*.

Uncle Gollu Mollu said that the middle finger in North America is like the left hand in Pakistan—you have it, but you're not supposed to use it. He said that when Tutoo and I are at school, we should never use the middle finger to scratch our noses or our chins.

Giant Uncle told us to buy a lot of socks. He said that in Canada, Canadians treat their toes like Pakistanis treat womens' chests—they always need to be kept covered.

Next-Door Uncle said that North Americans clean their backsides by using only toilet paper. They don't have bidets, squat toilets or lotas. They believe wiping their backside and smearing their caca with a piece of paper is enough. "They are a filthy people." He shuddered and warned us to never shake their hands.

Sibbi Phuppo cautioned us that North Americans only eat a single dish at a time. She told us to continue to eat like proper Pakistanis and have a variety of tastes and flavors at each mealtime. "Don't let your palates turn basic. And don't come back here moaning that black pepper tingles your tongue."

Bacha advised us to start learning French quickly, because it's the country's second official language and everyone learns it from birth and is fluent in it. He taught Tutoo how to introduce herself. "Bone chore, jay maple Tutoo." Tutoo practiced all afternoon.

Mithai-wallah told us that the winter in Canada is so cold that the temperature falls to forty below zero. He explained that in forty below zero, you get something called "frostbite," where the frost takes a bite out of your toes, and your toes turn black, then fall off. He told us that most Canadians have six or seven toes, eight at most, and that explains their obsession with socks.

Last but not least, Aba told us that schools are not closed for Fridays! Saturdays and Sundays will be our days off instead. While it sounds nice to have two days off every week, there is no time off for the two Eids or the Prophet's birthday or other religious holidays that I'm used to, and Canadian summer and winter holidays are shorter too. Tutoo added it all up in her head and subtracted where she needed to and concluded that we'll actually be getting *less* days off school! Out of all the things we learned today, this one was easily the most disturbing!

Sunday, August 4, 1991

I couldn't sleep last night. Who can I talk to about my worries about our move, ya Allah? Every grown-up around me just wants to talk about the electricity, the blackouts and where to buy fresh vegetables!

In the middle of the night, I wandered into the room where my parents sleep and I went to stand by Aba's side of the bed. I poked him in the ribs. He opened one eye. I whispered, "Aba, I don't want to go to Canada." He closed his eye and turned over. I pressed on bravely. "It's too cold, Aba. I've studied the temperatures in the almanac. The last fifty years have not been good. Aba. Aba. Aba." He groaned. "Aba, my eyelids are going to freeze shut every night. I'll likely lose two toes. Maybe even a finger."

Aba took a deep breath and turned back over to face me in the darkness.

"Mona, great change brings great growth . . ."

"Great change brings what?" I whispered grumpily.

"Growth. *Growth*. It brings growth." He grunted.

I was stunned. It was like I barely knew my father. Who was this man? Had we grown up on two different planets? Didn't he know that moving to a new world would destroy my life? Didn't he care one whit for me?

"Mona, my pearl, it will be a world with new stories. Our newspapers don't tell all the stories. Not here in Pakistan and not in the UAE either. Don't you want to live in a world where we can hear different stories?" he mumbled into the darkness, his eyes still shut.

My mind reeled. I didn't know if I did. What would such a world be like?

Aba muttered on. "Hasn't our friend Cousteau told us, '*Il faut aller voir*'?"

Monday, August 5, 1991

I couldn't sleep again last night, so this time I wandered in the dark toward Jibbi Phuppo. She's now officially married but is still living at Dadi's until we leave (since Aba is her favorite brother, after all). Jibbi Phuppo was in the living room, lying back on the wicker rocking chair with a beauty mask on her face. Her eyes were shut. Her shoulders jerked when I announced, "It's me, Mona," and that I couldn't sleep.

"Oh, it's you, Mona . . . go back to bed."

"I'm scared, Jibbi Phuppo."

"Is it Sibbi with those jinn stories again? I've told her to stop."

"It's not that. It's . . . I don't want to move to Canada."

"Mona, life is full of changes. You grow in all the right ways when you do the things that terrify you."

"But what if I don't want to grow in all the right ways? Can't I stay eleven? Next-Door Uncle's wife has been saying she's twenty-five for the last five years."

"Mona, big girls don't cry at night about moving to countries with working electricity. Who in their right mind would be scared of comfort? Go to bed."

"I have comfort in Dubai, Phuppo. Lots of it. Why can't we stay there?"

"Ya Allah, am I to be without a moment of peace, even at the end of the day?"

"Are you getting pretty for Motorcycle Uncle?"

"Mona, go to bed."

"Mithai-wallah told us we're going to lose our toes in the winter."

"Ya Allah, give me patience. Mona, if you come out of the bedroom one more time . . ."

"But frostbite—"

"One. More. Time . . . and Mona, no one needs all ten toes anyway."

Tuesday, August 6, 1991

The grown-ups are taking us to a hair salon tomorrow. We are all getting haircuts, and I've chosen the haircut I'm getting for my new life! It's from a picture of a woman from one of Ami's magazines. The woman in the picture is pushing a grocery cart. The cart is loaded with fruits and vegetables and a slim box of Kotex. There's a dusting of snow on the ground—it looks like she's in Canada. She's walking toward the parking lot, and she has car keys in her hand. She has all ten fingers pushing the cart, and her eight toes are hidden in her brown boots that almost reach her knees. There's no father, uncle or husband with her. She's getting her groceries alone. I don't know who is going to be her hero against the bad guys! It looks like she's driving by herself too. Where is she going? Anywhere she wants, I guess. She has a short man-haircut. There's a French word for it. *Chic*—c-h-i-c.

I've decided that that's the haircut I'm going to get tomorrow! I ripped the picture out of the magazine when Ami was sleeping and later swore that I saw Bibi do it. Tomorrow I'll ask for this man-haircut for my new life in Canada. It'll help me blend in like all the other pale-skinned, brave women in magazines.

Wednesday, August 7, 1991

11:00 a.m. No. No. No. No. NO! The Hair Salon Auntie looked and looked at the magazine picture, then snipped and snipped, but it's come out all wrong!

My short hair doesn't lie down flat and *chic* like in the picture! Even though Ami promises it's not that bad, I can clearly see that she's lying and that it's frizzy and wiry and decidedly *not* chic!

Will Canada even let me in? I don't match my passport picture at all!

2:00 p.m. We just got back from the doctor's office, where we had to have all our shots for Canada. In the waiting room, I noticed that everyone was looking at me strange. It's because of my haircut, of course.

3:00 p.m. I'm going to take scissors to it and fix it up a bit.

3:30 p.m. No. No. No. No. No. No. No. No. No. No. No. No. No. No. No. No. No. No. No. No. No. No. No. No. No. No. No. No. No. No. No. No. No. No. No. No. No. No. No. No. No. No. No. No. No. No. No. *Nooooooooooooooooooooooo!*

4:00 p.m. Have a plan! I'm a genius.

4:30 p.m. I'm becoming a hijabi. Starting tomorrow morning!

Thursday, August 8, 1991

I came out of the bedroom this morning with my headscarf wrapped around my hair. Dadi almost choked on her samosa and dropped her chai.

According to Dadi, a woman should be modest but not *too* modest. T-shirts, pants *and* headscarves are all out! No one on my father's side wears a hijab. There are families that are the hijabi families and families that are the not-hijabi families. We are one of the not-hijabi families, so it's difficult for me to do something that no one in my family has ever done before. All the grown-ups in my family are looking at me like I just grew a third eye. My cousins and sister, however, don't understand what the big deal is.

Before bedtime, Dadi lectured that there was no point wearing a hijab if the rest of me was in a T-shirt and pants, or if I was still going to run around playing cricket outside, or if I was going to tie the cloth in a big knot at the back of my neck and show off the skin at the front. "If you're going to be a hijabi, then live the full hijabi way. Don't wear pants. Don't play sports. Don't show off your neck skin."

Does it matter, Allah? Don't You think that if I can break the rules in my not-hijabi family by wearing a scarf, then I can also break the other rules about how to tie it, the clothes to wear with it and the games to play in it?

Friday, August 9, 1991

During our morning game of cricket, we planted three long sticks in the ground for the wicket. Bachee was wicket-keeper and I was the batsman. Bachee caught a ball that had nicked my bat, and as she did so, running up behind me, her bangles got caught in the tassels of my scarf. When she moved away, my scarf was yanked off my head. It was humiliating because everyone saw my sweaty hair matted to my skull!

Later while running past Bachee, I reached out and pinched her on the arm. "But it wasn't on purpose, Mona!" she screamed. I shrugged and pinched her other arm. Bachee sighed in exasperation. On the way home, she complained, "Uff. You're just as troublesome as you've always been, Mona. You haven't changed a bit with a scarf on!"

What a silly cousin I have! Of course I'm the same old me—why would a piece of cloth change anything?

Saturday, August 10, 1991

Dadi keeps asking me to change my mind about the hijab. "Don't you want to blend in? Why stand out in life?"

Why won't she leave me alone?! I bet you no one in Canada will bother me about the clothes on my body!

Tonight is our last night in Isloo. We go back to Dubai tomorrow. CAPITAL S for SAD that summer is almost over, but CAPITAL G for GLAD that I can be somewhere without Dadi's nagging!

Sunday, August 11, 1991

The whole world came to the airport. At the airport, Dadi made a big scene and sobbed loudly. Why must grandmothers cry so loudly? Probably something to do with knowing death is around the corner.

The cousins made a going-away card for Tutoo and me. They wrote a short poem inside—

> *We wish you a world of new choices.*
> *Remember us and don't forget our voices.*

There was something stuck in my eyes the whole flight and they wouldn't stop watering.

Monday, August 12, 1991

Back in comfortable, big city, AC-full Dubai.

Even though my mother's waddling around with a basketball-shaped tummy and taking the longest naps in the universe, she did manage to arrange a goodbye party for tonight. She got on the phone and told one person, who told another person, who told the next and so on, until everyone we love showed up at our apartment with food and farewell hugs. No one said "goodbye"—they all said "see you later," which means even grown-ups understand that sometimes lying is necessary.

Also, I am noting that no one got me a gift. But almost everyone asked me about my headscarf. "Good for you," some of my loved ones said. "Such a shame," the others tsked. Everyone had an opinion on my headscarf but no one had the common sense or decency to keep it to themselves! And here I've been kindly biting my tongue on their fashion choices my entire life.

Why can't they just let me be eleven and figure it out? At what age do grown-ups stop figuring it out?

Laila was the only one who seemed to get it. Standing in her goth-attire, she looked me up and down, approvingly. "Punk, Mona," she finally said, giving me a sign of the horns, which I think is something important in goth language.

Whether by hook or by crook, Laila and I promised to find a way back to each other for each other's graduations and weddings and first babies.

Tuesday, August 13, 1991

Our new life in Canada will start any day now because according to Aba, the "visa" from Canada is coming any day now.

Wednesday, August 14, 1991

Any day.

Thursday, August 15, 1991

Any day.

Friday, August 16, 1991

Not today.

Saturday, August 17, 1991

Nor today.

Sunday, August 18, 1991

Not yet.

Monday, August 19, 1991

Nope.

Tuesday, August 20, 1991

Sigh.

Wednesday, August 21, 1991

The thing is, no one knows when the visa will come, so there's no point in waking up and wanting for today to be that day. But it *IS* the only thing we wonder about, and Aba already said goodbye to his job in Dubai and is now sitting around boring us all with facts on marine plants and animals. Oh Allah, please hurry!

Thursday, August 22, 1991

When Aba saw the mailman in the parking lot making his way over into our building with a large manila envelope, Aba ran to the fridge and grabbed a box of mithai. Aba, Tutoo and I hightailed it to the elevator, where my scarf almost got caught in the closing doors and I almost lost my head! We carried on and rushed into the lobby in our bare feet to greet the startled mailman!

Aba fed the mailman our best pieces of mithai with his hands.

Our papers for Canada have finally arrived!

Friday, August 23, 1991

Ami tucked little packets of masala into the sides of all our bulging suitcases. Tutoo and I packed all our most precious belongings into our backpacks, and we put the rest into boxes that will go into a storage room and come to Canada later. All our favorite stuffies and dolls, our summer sandals and beach hats and dresses. Oh, and all the drafts of my poems that I keep under my mattress—I moved all of these into a cardboard box marked DO NOT TOUCH UPON PAIN OF GREVIOUS INJURY BY MONA HASAN—MONA HASAN'S WORLDLY TREASURES CIRCA 1991. I placed my birthday cards and letters and postcards from friends on the top. My handmade bookmarks! My stamp collection! My pressed-leaf collection! My coins from around the world, and all the classroom notes passed and shared with secrets and squiggles and hearts, and that slightly torn, very crumpled paper swan! I nestled it all delicately into the cardboard box and taped the top.

Ami says that when we get to Canada, we'll buy whatever we've forgotten or left behind. Of course. Of course, anything that has been left behind is something that can be replaced and bought in a Canadian shop.

Saturday, August 24, 1991

I have decided not to take my diary on our flight to Toronto, Canada, and I will pack it in a suitcase instead. I cannot be certain that it will not be read by nosy eyes (I HOPE TUTOO HAS NOT BEEN READING MY DIARY. DEAR TUTOO—YOU SHOULD NOT READ MY

DIARY! IT IS PERSONAL, WITH PRIVATE, SOPHISTICATED GROWN-UP STUFF THAT IS *NOT* YOUR BUSINESS! STOP NOW!!).

Besides, my diary doesn't fit into my COOL, bejeweled Teenage Mutant Ninja Turtle–shaped purse.

Sunday, August 25, 1991

Monday, August 26, 1991

FINALLY THE HASANS HAVE ARRIVED in Canada!

And You, Allah? What about You? Are You here too?

We took a yellow cab from the Mr. Lester B. Pearson airport to a place in Toronto called "Scarbo-ruff." The taxi driver told Aba its pronounced "Scarbo-*ro*"! My father tried to explain to the poor man that it's spelled "rough" like "tough," but the taxi driver wouldn't listen. "It's not his fault," Aba whispered to us afterwards. "He probably didn't do his homework—that's why he's ended up a taxi driver." But then the word came up on the radio, and the taxi driver snapped his fingers and nodded his head up and down. Aba looked horrified and gave a sheepish smile to us in the back!

Tuesday, August 27, 1991

We're staying with a second cousin of a second cousin on my mother's side. Someone we've never met before. His name is Uncle Ali. Uncle Ali welcomed us warmly into his one-bedroom, one-bathroom apartment and told us we could stay for as long as we need. "Three weeks or three years," he said and stretched his arms out from his sides, hitting the walls on either side of him.

Uncle Ali lives on the third floor of a boxy twelve-floor building. There are a lot of families who live in this building, and there is a lot of noise. We hear babies crying at all hours, and toddlers are always running up and down the hallways. Inside, his tiny place is cluttered and cramped. He keeps the radio set to an Indian music station to drown out the outside clamor.

On the ledge of his kitchen window, Uncle Ali keeps an uncovered Holy Quran pressed next to a copy of the Torah.

After dinner Uncle Ali told us the story of when he came to Canada.

"I came in '58, when Canada was giving out foreign student visas like lollipops. The jobs they weren't giving out so easily, but you know, I haven't done too badly here. Half the paycheck I've been sending home since '65, when my Amijaan had that gallbladder thing, you remember, and the other half has given me enough to be comfortable. More than comfortable, really. I am proud of this country. They can take as much as they bloody want from me in taxes. Leave me enough for food and love, and I'll happily leave this world with zero complaints. Zero savings and zero complaints."

Scarborough by Mona Hasan, 11¾
We're here in Scarbo-rough
Without any stuff
Uncle said, "If you're going to wear that fluff
on the top of your head, then you have to be tough,"
But I'm just happy it hides my dandruff

Wednesday, August 28, 1991

Our parents spent most of today like the other days—fretting and scolding one moment, then mouths open and eyes shut on the sofa the next. They complained about jet lag, bad backs, pinching games and migraines.

1. Wake up.
2. Brush your teeth.
3. Eat your food.
4. Sit up straight.
5. Talk to your uncle.
6. Stop bothering your uncle.
7. Get out of your pajamas.
8. Get into your pajamas.
9. Brush your teeth.
10. Go to sleep.

It rains in Dubai once, maybe twice a year! But it's been raining in Toronto all week!

The days here are a blur of gray. Is it early morning? Early evening? Who can tell? The buildings, the roads, the sky, the trees, the cars, peoples' jackets, their pants, their boots. And even their faces. All basically mottled gray.

I woke up early, before anyone else, and locked myself in the washroom for a moment of quiet. I looked in the mirror. My chest was still flat! My face was a small, round ball of mottled mud. I missed my cousins. My aunts. My uncles. Dadi. Laila. Mrs. Naz. Waleed, even. Maryam too. Will I ever make any friends here? How? When?

In the middle of my loneliness, Tutoo pounded on the door saying she needed to poo.

Thursday, August 29, 1991

Uncle Ali's tiny one-bedroom, one-bathroom apartment contains:

1. Uncle Ali
2. Aba
3. Ami
4. Tutoo
5. Me
6. Pierre Trudeau

Pierre Trudeau is Uncle Ali's chunky orange-and-white goldfish, and Tutoo's already fallen in love with him. Uncle Ali is allowing Tutoo to feed him every morning, which means Pierre Trudeau will be belly-up in no time.

I can hear the pipes when the neighbors shower or flush. I hear when they come home from work, when they drop something on the floor and when they're angry with each other. How long before we can go to our own home, Allah?

Friday, August 30, 1991

After breakfast. EXCITEMENT! Uncle Ali is taking all of us to a store called Value Village so we can buy clothes for our first Canadian winter! We are going to look so *COOL* on our first day of SCHOOL!

Later that evening. I had to buy a hideous purple snow jacket! I wanted a pretty navy-blue one to match my headscarf but the store didn't have one in my size.

"Can't we go to a store with more sizes and colors, Aba?"

"Do you have any idea what the exchange rate is for the UAE dirhams to Canadian dollars?"

"No."

"You take the money I had in Dubai, and you divide it by three."

"Oh."

"Now you know how much money we have for life in Canada."

"Oh."

There's no War in Canada, but with all this worrying about money, there's not quite Peace either, is there, Allah?

CHAPTER NINE

September

Sunday, September 1, 1991

Canada is so quiet! After the after-school specials, there is so much silence outside that it's almost deafening! Where are all the Canadians? Don't they know we have arrived and want to practice our English?

Monday, September 2, 1991

This morning Uncle Ali gathered us in the kitchen where his linoleum is peeling, his counters are a dusty pink, and all his plates are either mismatched or chipped. He fussed about the direction of the light and directed us to our positions and poses and reminded us we only had one take to get it right, so I kept my eyelids open until my eyes watered.

There was a loud click and a sharp white light. A small white square ejected slowly from his camera. He rummaged through his drawers, found a black Sharpie and wrote, "Hasans—Toronto, '91" in fancy script along the bottom of the Polaroid.

"This will mean something many years from now," he promised Tutoo, and she flapped the Polaroid dry, then tucked it into her kitty purse for safekeeping.

I'll have to make sure Tutoo loses that photo! Not only did Uncle Ali make us wear our hideous winter jackets in his hot kitchen, but the camera also captured Tutoo with both hands on her hips in an adventurous superhero triangle pose, while I was caught slouching in the back with bulging bug eyes and a grimace.

Tuesday, September 3, 1991

Uncle Ali explained important things about Canada today. Aba sat at his feet, jotted notes on a yellow legal pad and tried to ask intelligent-sounding questions.

If Uncle Ali is to be believed:

1. Every year, the leaves on the trees are going to go from green to yellow to red.
2. Public buses and trains are so safe that women and children can go on them without men to protect them.

3. Public libraries give out books for free and expect you to return them because you make a promise to do so.

Uncle Ali mentioned some other stuff too, but these seemed like the most important.

Wednesday, September 4, 1991

The parents went for their driving tests today. Ami passed hers but Aba failed his. He didn't know that pedestrians have something called "right of way."

Thursday, September 5, 1991

Aba is going to spend tomorrow standing in lines for our PR, or Permanent Resident, cards *and* health cards *and* bank cards and all the other cards you need to live in Canada. Hopefully he'll get those library cards soon too so I can start stealing some books.

Ami's tummy is as big as a giant watermelon now. She's going to stay home as much as she can and do the woman-things. Soap operas. Dishes. You know.

Uncle Ali said he's going to call in sick tomorrow so that he can help Tutoo and me fall in love with our new country.

Friday, September 6, 1991

Uncle Ali, Tutoo and I piled into a rickety-looking train, or "streetcar," and it rattled for an hour all the way west to Toronto's downtown. The place was a bleak collection of battered, low buildings and it was practically a ghost town. Not at all like Dubai's skyline! Despite all this, Uncle Ali beamed, pointing out the sights with the same pride as a tour guide showing us the pyramids of Giza.

On the way back, we stood on an open platform that looked like a public urinal. We were waiting for the streetcar east when a group of college-age Canadians on the other side of the platform started waving and yelling at us. One of them shouted, "Hey, Pakis, go home!"

Tutoo and I waved back excitedly. Later, Uncle Ali said he didn't get it either—how did those boys know exactly where we were headed, Allah?

Saturday, September 7, 1991

Uncle Ali made dinner for us tonight. He baked whitefish, which he drizzled with olive oil and sprinkled with sea salt. Then he boiled some potatoes and steamed some carrots and broccoli. Just as Sibbo Phuppo had warned us, the only "flourishes" he added were salt and pepper. "Canadian food for my soon-to-be Canadians!" he said and sat the fish in the middle of the table. We politely nibbled at our dinner. Later Ami confessed to him that she was amazed an entire meal could be prepared with so few spices. Aba confessed that he was amazed an entire meal could be prepared by a man!

Sunday, September 8, 1991

My parents have been up late talking every night. Tutoo and I pretend to be asleep. Aba says he would like Tutoo and me to start school right away, but Uncle Ali warned him that public school in Toronto may not be the best launching pad for young Muslim girls from Dubai.

"The problem is that soon you will have two teenage girls on your hands. This is Toronto. Big city, big city problems. The Tamil boys are in gangs. The Hindu boys are in gangs. One or two of our Sunni boys are also going astray. The girls get swallowed up with a gang boy, then boom. Gone! All your hard work. Poof. Into thin air. Listen to me. Who have I not advised? Hameed and family, I settled them nicely in Calgary. Now they're happy, doing fine. Shabnum and family—I advised them to go back. That was right decision for them. Jumshaid—I sent to Winnipeg. You? You should go to Halifax. I am telling you, property prices are low and community life is good. Perfect place for two teenage girls. Soon you will have new baby. Best you get healthy ocean air into new-baby lungs. I have the perfect business venture for you. My boss has a brother-in-law who has a friend who has a cousin, and that good man is selling a gas station. He will give to you at perfect price. It's in small town but so what? These city folk, the dream is to retire in small town, so you go there first. Beat them to it, as they say. Or is it just "beat them"? Anyway, you are from Middle East. Why you should not be in oil business? *O-ho*, you do this for a few months—one, two years tops—*then* you will have the 'Canadian experience' as they say. *Then* you apply for banking jobs. Great plan, no?

Also, in small city your daughters will have zero competition for universities and for those ABCD tests. When the time comes, lead your daughters by the ears and make sure they write one of those alphabet tests—the MCAT, the GMAT or the LSAT. If your daughters ace any of those ABCD tests, then this whole citizenship gamble . . . jackpot.

Arrey yaar, you don't want your children to be wiping down toilet bowls like us, do you? Oh no, no, that's not what I meant. Yes, yes, of course you'll find something in banking sector in Halifax. Why not? You speak English well. Very bloody wells. Like me. I am doing very fine, am I not? But the future for you—bright like light bulb. You know A-one languages for banks in Halifax! Every bank needs expert from Middle East. They will be hiring you fatafat fast! Watch how the phone will be ringing off the hook for you.

Be trusting me, go to Halifax. Settle there. Property prices are low but sure to go up later. All kinds of jobs opening there. It's *emerging* city. Toronto is pile of decaying rubble and soot—only a crazy man would bet on this city. Everyone in Toronto wants to leave this pile of . . . not at all good for family life. Best you go east or west. I am telling you, Canada's center is a crazy-man's gamble."

Monday, September 9, 1991

Aba bought a minivan from Uncle Ali's boss's brother-in-law. Ami's going to drive it to this city called Halifax, in a peninsula province called Nova Scotia, on the east coast of Canada. To get there we just have to drive along a highway called the Trans-Canada Highway. The route from Toronto to Halifax is only 1,800 kilometers, which could be a two-day trip if we drove all day, but the grown-ups mapped it out with some rest-stops and detours, and we're planning on being there in four days instead. At our small town rest-stops, we just have to watch out for pedestrians and obey all the traffic lights. Uncle Ali says we are lucky that at this time of year there also isn't something called "black ice" to contend with. How hard can this drive be?

Tutoo had to wail and blubber for forty-seven minutes, then lie down dead in the living room for another seventeen minutes, but finally Uncle Ali gifted Pierre Trudeau to us. We fit the goldfish bowl into a square cardboard box and wedged the box snugly behind the driver's seat. Aba, Ami, Tutoo, me, Pierre Trudeau and the one-half in Ami's tummy are OFF! Wish us luck.

Halifax by Mona Hasan, 11¾

This new country collects tax,

Has a lot of Jills and a lot of Jacks!

We've squished as much as we could into our
backpacks,

We've bundled up Pierre Trudeau, as well as
some spicy snacks.

We're following Trans-Canada Highway east
for the climax—

Our new lives in Halifax!

Tuesday, September 10, 1991

During the stretch between Toronto and Quebec City, Ami told us a story while she drove with one sun-darkened hand on the steering wheel.

"A long, long time ago, in a land now far, far away, there was one big, beautiful, confusing country called India. Muslims and Hindus and Sikhs and Buddhists and Parsis and Christians and Jews and Ahmedis and atheists and cows and donkeys and monkeys all lived side by side. Sure, there were small hiccups here and there, but families were big and colorful, and we looked each other eye in the beautiful eye. The British came and messed this all up. They got sun-burned, stole jewels, made babies and drew borders. We can't blame only the British for how the subcontinent is today, but we can mostly blame them because the night they left, they made black marks on maps and a Great Partition had to happen. That night India split into two—India and Pakistan. My parents moved into the new part of old India—Pakistan. It was often chaotic. Unstable. Twenty-five years later, there was another split—Pakistan split into old Pakistan and Bangladesh. More problems happened. More instability. This time my family decided to stay in old Pakistan as everyone around us left. Your father's family came and settled across the train tracks. We locked eyes. Married. Left for a new life in Dubai.

In Dubai, Aba had no money and no connections. Aba was twenty-four and I was nineteen. Today Aba is thirty-six and I'm thirty-one. And again we've left everything behind for a new world.

But it worked out back then, with much less money in our pockets. And it's all going to work out again. It's going to be okay."

When you are eleven-turning-twelve, the most comforting words to hear in the world are "it's going to be okay."

Wednesday, September 11, 1991

Almost there. We reached a province called New Brunswick today. There sure is a lot of nature around here. We didn't know where to stop to take pictures—everything on this side of the country is so full of natural wonder and beauty that we decided not to take any pictures at all.

We stopped at a roadside restaurant to eat. Over the local delicacy of potatoes, gravy and cheese curds, Aba told Tutoo and me that he has bought a small gas station. He promised Ami, Tutoo and me that by day, he will work at the gas station, and by night he will look for a job in Nova Scotia's thriving international banking sector.

When we got back in the car, Aba told me that I can also put in some shifts with him at the gas station too.

Thursday, September 12, 1991

ARRIVED!

And Pierre Trudeau made it too! He's alive and now has pride of place in the middle of our living room.

We are renting a two-bedroom apartment in a "stepping stone" apartment complex called Lakecrest Apartments, which is in a small town called Dartmouth, about fifteen minutes from the big city, Halifax. Aba says that small-town life will be more fun because it will be slower, friendlier and less expensive! I'm sure it won't be all that different from my life in Dubai—kids anywhere are the same as kids everywhere, right?

Aba reassured us that this "stepping stone" building has been the first home of many, many Canadian newcomers! From here successful newcomers have gone on to live in posher neighborhoods like Portland Estates and Montebello, and I'm sure that that's where we'll end up too, right, Allah? Aba spent a long time explaining that this is just a "starter" place, but he completely failed to understand the real dilemma for Tutoo and me: We have to share a bedroom for the first time in our lives! The only good thing is that this is a step up from all of us sleeping in Uncle Ali's living room.

Tutoo and I dumped our stuff into our small bedroom and surveyed our new kingdoms. I drew a line on the carpet with my toe and claimed the slightly bigger half.

Outside our bedroom window, there is a dark shady area that the locals call the "woods." The "woods" lie beyond the parking lot, beyond the dumpsters, and I swear I heard some wolves howling from over there but maybe that was just the neighbors flushing.

We don't have beds yet, but we bought comforters and pillows and laid them on the floor. For our first night in Dartmouth, I have a pillow, a pen and paper. The rest is just details.

I'm writing in my diary right now and Tutoo just asked me, "Aren't you scared, Mona?" Tutoo is looking out the window. It's dark and cold out there. I don't know what to say and Tutoo pushes on. "You're brave all the time, aren't you, Mona? Aren't ever you scared of anything?"

I know what Tutoo is thinking. That there are monsters out there in the cold. And sometimes the monsters are closer to home. I tell Tutoo that I'm terrified too, but that the trick I use is that I make my hopes bigger than my fears. I tell Tutoo that in one year, we're going to plaster our bedroom wall with photos of all the friends we have made and all the new places we have seen. Places like Shubie Park, Peggy's Cove, Lawrencetown Beach, The Hawk, Bay of Fundy, Gros Morne, Greenwich Dunes . . . and the best ones are the ones without any names attached to them at all. We'll see landscapes so stunning that we'll be too awed to be fearful. I also write her a poem—

Hope by Mona Hasan, 11¾
Hope is the thing that is dope
Though a gale may blow, don't mope
Just cope
Plant hope
It's dope

Friday, September 13, 1991

By sharing a bedroom, Tutoo and I are really bonding.

At breakfast Tutoo looked up at me dreamily.

"Baji, remember when we were younger and we used to play games for hours? Then sometime in grade five, you became this total stranger who ran from me every time I came near you, like I had a horrible disease? Can we be best friends now that I'm the only one you know in this country?"

"Stop staring at me, Tutoo. And chew with your mouth closed. I can see all your food. Gross."

"You don't have any friends here either, Baji. You'll have to be my friend now, won't you?"

"We won't be the new kids for the rest of our lives."

"Do you really think I'm just a stinky little sister?"

"You stink less when you are quiet."

That finally shut up her blathering.

Ya Allah, I'd better make friends at school ASAP, otherwise I'll be stuck playing hand-clapping games with Tutoo until I'm a hundred.

Saturday, September 14, 1991

While Aba went to the closest grocery store to get some necessities, Ami and I met our neighbor from across the hall—Mrs. Rousopoulos. Mrs. Rousopoulos is very loud, very curvy, and did I already mention her loud, booming laugh? She lives alone with her daughter, who is Tutoo's age. The daughter's name is Sofia. Sofia has yellow hair that she chews nervously. She has her own bedroom.

Mrs. Rousopoulos and Sofia came over with muffins that they'd bought from a store. My mother invited them in for tea. Sofia and Tutoo bounded off to our bedroom to play, and I loitered in the kitchen where I heard my mother and Mrs. Rousopoulos discuss the best playgrounds, the cheapest grocery stores and registration for school. After an hour, my mother said my father would be home soon and that she must tidy up, prepare a hot meal, and boil a fresh cup of chai for his arrival. Mrs. Rousopoulos looked at my mother, stunned, and inquired politely, "Why, does he not have arms?"

My mother stared back at Mrs. Rousopoulos blankly. Long seconds passed in mutual confusion. Then Mrs. Rousopoulos excused herself and said, "Well, I'd better get back to the novel I've been working on for the last ten years. It's an excuse to shirk domestic drudgery, really." She inhaled two of my mother's homemade samosas, smiled sweetly and left.

My mother watched Mrs. Rousopoulos leave—rather wistfully, I noticed.

Sunday, September 15, 1991

On the way home from dropping off laundry at the laundromat, my father and I bumped into Mrs. Rousopoulos in the mailroom. Mrs. Rousopoulos advanced toward my father, confidently extending her right palm and asking his name.

"Haider," my father said proudly.

"Yes, hi there," Mrs. Rousopoulos repeated.

"No, my *name* is Haider."

"Heather?" she asked, eyebrows arching.

"Hai*der*," he repeated.

"Hea*ther*," she returned politely.

"No, no. My name is being Haider," my father clarified.

"Ah. Your name is *bin Heather*." She smiled proudly.

"*Der, der.* Haider," my father grunted, painfully aware that his name was being mangled into a woman's name.

They danced around their pronunciation confusion a few more times, and I saw my father's shoulders go from straight to slumped. He muttered a bad word under his breath, cradled the jumbo-sized bottle of detergent tighter and walked stiffly back into our unit.

Monday, September 16, 1991

Furniture has been ordered, and some rickety study tables for Tutoo and I were bought and assembled by Aba today.

Now that we are all settled in, my parents want to register us at the local school. We are going to enter the esteemed Canadian public education system! "There'll be an adjustment period. The schools here might be slightly different," Aba said worriedly. How different can school be here, right, Allah?

Tutoo and I are going to two separate schools. She's going to Caledonia *Elementary* School, which is a ten-minute walk toward the west, and I'll be at John A. Macdonald *Junior High* School, which is a ten-minute walk to the east. John A. Macdonald School was named for a dead-important actual dead man who either started many wars or accumulated a lot of land—either of which is obviously a marker of a life well-lived.

Aba and Ami took us for a drive, and we circled both schools a few times in our white van until we noticed that the teachers in the playground were giving us nervous looks, so we drove off to circle Aba's new gas station instead.

Tutoo's school had some colorful murals on its walls, and the kids were outside skipping rope. Tutoo even spotted Sofia in the playground! On the other hand, my school looked like a prison building. Not a soul in the schoolyard. The red-brick building was boxy and rectangular with small windows.

Tomorrow we're going for registration.

Tuesday, September 17, 1991

John A. Macdonald Junior High—the inside was all shiny floors and bright lights. The principal assured us that the school is a bastion of the Canadian education system. It appears that I will be SO MUCH smarter once I've been through Canada's esteemed public school system! Will the world be ready for my brilliance?!!

Ami filled out all the paperwork at the office. After she was done filling forms and signing signatures, she cracked her knuckles nervously. "Everything okay here, right? The kids are . . . *friendly?*"

The school secretary (her nameplate read MS. CHARLOTTE McLEAN) looked up at Ami sweetly. Walked over from her desk and embraced my mother in a side hug.

"Go on, love. You're not in Cole Harbour, are yah, eh? You're on the right side of the tracks here. You'll be some happy ter know that we have lots and lots of Come From Aways here in Dartmouth. The Lebanese particularly have been swarmin' in here since the mid-sixties. In this school alone, there are *three*, if you can believe it! Seif—he goes by Sam; Moortaza—he goes by Matt; and Muhammed—we call 'im Moe, don't we?

She'll have that Middle Eastern, Muslim connection with those three and they'll be right thrilled ter meet her, won't they? There'll just be *SO* much for them all ter talk about! Well, Moe's actually from Malaysia, and Sam's not actually Muslim . . . Coptic Christian, he says, and no one knows exactly where Matt's parents came from, he keeps tight lips about that. Minor details, love. They *do* all have that third-world connection with each other, don't they? *Third-world?* Jumpin' Jesus, that's not very politically correct anymore, is it? What I meant is that they're all some foreign, so of course they'll all be fast friends. Bring her back down here right at half past noon tomorrow. I'll ask Sam ter give 'er a tour of the school, eh. It's gonna be okay, love."

She wrote down "Wednesday, 12:30" on a sticky note. We had a long family discussion about it and we're pretty sure it means I'm supposed to go back tomorrow at twelve thirty. Wish me luck!

Wednesday, September 18, 1991

I've already missed the first two weeks of grade seven but no need to worry—a *late* entrance always makes for a *great* entrance. I'll stand out memorably, which I suppose is exactly what a new girl needs to do in seventh grade! I've already picked out my first-day outfit—gold tights, a shalwar hand-embroidered by Dadi and my favorite headscarf! Dartmouth, I'm ready!

First, I met "Sam" at the bottom of the stairs. He gave me a quiet tour of the tiny school, pointing out the important spaces.

The two rooms that caught my attention were:

1. The cafeteria. It smelled like chicken and soggy cardboard. I am definitely packing my own lunches!
2. The art room. There were paint splatters on every surface. Messy tins of linseed oil and tubes of oil paint were on the floor, but somehow the chaos felt soothing.

After "Sam" was done with the tour (and after calculating my odds and concluding that he most likely cleaned his backside in the proper ways of the Old Country), I extended my hand for a handshake, just like I had seen Mrs. Rousopoulos do.

"See you at lunchtime tomorrow, then," I offered generously. He looked down at my palm and recoiled. Exhaled noisily. "Listen, me and my boys were born here." I blinked back blankly. He sighed. "We have piano after school and play ice hockey at the local rink. Don't you get it? I made the football team this year and might even have a chance to score with a Canadian girl. Don't say hi to me in the hallways and absolutely never, *ever* sit down for lunch with me and my boys." I heard him mutter, "My parents are embarrassing enough," then he bolted down the hallway.

I haven't a clue what he meant by his words, Allah! It's interesting that he's going to score goals with a Canadian girl on his football team, but I have no idea why he needed to tell me that! I guess we can't spend lunchtime together because boys and girls don't mingle much here either. I must find some friendly girls instead.

Thursday, September 19, 1991

Aba took Tutoo and me to his gas station today. There's a little store attached to it where he's selling food wrapped in plastic. We've noticed that it's very important for Canadians to have food without any smells. Tutoo and I walked around and studied all the different packages of chips and candy bars and gum. What we couldn't touch were the things behind the cash desk—cigarettes and lottery tickets.

The previous owner, Mr. Baliki, came to the store to share tips and stories with Aba. His cousin's friend's nephew will split shifts with Aba for the next couple of months, or maybe a year or two, tops. Mr. Baliki showed Aba all the buttons that Aba needed to know. There were buttons for opening the lights, for unlocking the back room, for releasing the vault and the underground fuel barrels. There was also a big red button hidden under the cash register. "You press this one if there's any trouble." Tutoo and I gawked at the flimsy red plastic button. "How will a button help us if there's trouble?" Tutoo asked. Mr. Baliki looked surprised, then he shrugged cheerfully. "The important thing is to press it quickly," he answered. "Have you ever used it?" asked Tutoo. "No, but I've swung this around," and he pulled out a cricket bat that was tucked under a shelf on the cash register side. Since cricket bats were familiar to us, we instantly felt relieved.

"Most people come in here for emergency supplies like snow brushes or windshield wiper fluid," Mr. Baliki told Aba as we were leaving. "But late at night or during the lunch hour, people will also rush in for these." His eyebrows shot up. In one hand, he held up a blue box that read a Mystery Word, "TAMPONS," and from the other hand, he unfurled a strip of shiny plastic squares, each one printed with another new Mystery Word—"CONDOM."

Friday, September 20, 1991

We called Dadi today in Pakistan. All of us huddled around the phone in the living room as we placed the call on speaker.

Before the phone call, Aba took Tutoo and I aside and explained to us that he was going to play a trick on Dadi— "We're going to pretend that we're calling her from the future, okay? We're already living in our dream home. You both have your own bedrooms. There's a garden out front and one in the back. You were both out riding your bikes today. You played in the front yard with the neighbors' kids. Your mother planted some flowers in the garden. Tulips, okay? Ready?" Then he dialed his mother's number. Each of his siblings got a minute on the phone, and we could hear our cousins being shushed in the background.

At the end of Aba's spiel on our future-present, Dadi timidly asked, "So, you'll still be able to send us a little cash monthly? Oh, not as much as before, of course. Just a little top-up, you know. Taxes and utilities going up again this year." Aba inhaled sharply and before he could answer, Ami jumped in and retorted in an offended tone, "Of course, what kind of people do you think we are?" And everyone laughed nervously. At the end of the call, Dadi asked, "Canada is all you imagined and more?"

"Beyond our wildest dreams," Aba said and locked eyes with Ami. Then our parents said their goodbyes curtly and got off the phone as quickly as they could.

Saturday, September 21, 1991

I eavesdropped on the parents late at night. They were sitting on the sofa that had just been delivered that morning. My father had Mr. Baliki's old income tax papers and accountant reports strewn across the living room floor. Aba's head was in his hands.

"Applying under the investor program was a huge mistake. This country is going to bleed our savings dry. This isn't the life I planned for. I was the golden child in my family. I won all the math scholarships. I beat the odds. But now I've made a terrible mistake. Can you forgive me?"

"Enough with your melodrama, you old fart," Ami said. "I'm the one who pushed for this. I thought it would be better."

"Now what?"

"Now we wait for our children to save us."

Aba sighed, chuckled and pushed the papers under the sofa. "Yes, those magical rascals. They'll definitely rescue us," Aba muttered to Ami, and they turned off all the lights and turned in for bed.

What are we supposed to rescue our parents from, Allah? And how?

Sunday, September 22, 1991

It's our first day of school tomorrow and Aba's first shift at the gas station too! Ami is insisting on packing aloo parathas for Tutoo and me for lunch—"I'll pack an extra aloo paratha, and you can give it to one of the new friends you make at school."

Yeah, right. I've seen enough American movies set in high school to know that offering aloo paratha to anyone at school can only end in disaster.

When I get there, I'll just chuck the aloo parathas in the garbage—obviously the best way to make friends is to pretend that I'm someone else! Okay, World, here I come.

Monday, September 23, 1991

I begged and pleaded and laid down dead for fifty-seven minutes last night and finally Ami and I reached a compromise. I could walk to school alone as long as Ami could trail behind me creepily from a distance in the car. I didn't have to wave goodbye to her when I got to school, and she wasn't allowed to honk at me either.

My first class today was math—what good luck! The class was on chapter 3 (the division of fractions), which I'd already covered last year in Dubai! I made sure to answer all the questions the teacher asked, and I even demonstrated a complicated equation on the chalkboard at the front of the class. I just know by showing everyone how smart I am that I am going to make tons of new friends!

At lunchtime, no one approached me to strike up a friendship, so I read the math textbook by my locker. My stomach rumbled the whole time. On my first day of Canadian school, not only was I lonely at lunchtime but hungry too! It'll be a better day tomorrow, I'm sure of it!

Tuesday, September 24, 1991

Had classes with three men teachers—a soft-spoken science teacher (Mr. McNeil), a boisterous English teacher (Mr. D.), and a portly, jolly man (Mr. Barry), who is the gym teacher.

Mr. D. took one look at me walking into his classroom with a headscarf and spoke loudly.

"Oh dear. Do you speak Eeeeennggggllliiiisshhhh, sweetie?"

I calmly returned his stare.

"Yes, sir. It's one of the three languages I do speak. And you, do YOU speak Eeeeennggggllliiiisshhhh?"

Okay, no, I didn't do any of that. Instead, I stared at the dust on my shoes and meekly muttered, "A little, yes." Then I shuffled to my seat.

By the end of the day, I forgave Mr. D. his ignorance. After all, it must be embarrassing to be doing a woman's job.

Wednesday, September 25, 1991

Still reading my math textbook during lunchtime.

Why is no one approaching me to be my friend?!

Thursday, September 26, 1991

At lunchtime, Sam walked down the hallway with his *COOL* friends. I had to move my legs out of the way. He seemed to go to great lengths to avoid looking at me.

Friday, September 27, 1991

I have taken to sitting in the library for lunchtime. It is soothing in here. Also, I have finished my math textbook and after we had a quick chat, the kind librarian suggested I read a book series about a Canadian girl who also lived on the east coast of Canada and struggled to fit in. It's called the Anne of Green Gables series and there are nine books in all! "You can spend as many lunchtimes in here as you need," the librarian whispered quietly, and I had to turn my head because her kindness brought tears to my eyes.

Saturday, September 28, 1991

Dearest Laila,

How are you? How are your brothers? Your mom? Hala? Maryam? Mrs. Naz? Mrs. Adila? Mr. Qadri? Do tell me everything about everyone in exquisite detail. Of course, I have a queue of interesting new friends to choose from here, so please do not worry about me. I am not yet sure who I will choose to honor with best-friend status—but rest assured, it will be a tough choice! There is a girl with fiery red hair who chatters nonstop. Her name is Anne with an *e*, and I am thinking she might be The One!

In my Canadian classrooms, I sit side by side with boys and yes, it makes me a tad nervous. This summer, my cousin Bacha was kind enough to warn me that if you are alone in a room with a boy, then a baby will come. Thankfully Canadian classrooms in the public education system are pretty crowded, so I am never quite alone.

Life here is grand indeed. I ride my red bike to school, and for lunchtime I eat white bread sandwiches. Are you still having labneh with za'atar and olive oil every morning? Warm pita bread? Eggs scrambled with tomatoes and garnished with fresh parsley? Freshly squeezed fruit juices from Bilal's?

Oh, none of that peasant food for us here! A cold bowl of milk and dry North American cereal is what we have for breakfast, like in all the commercials. Mealtimes are not wasted in savoring. For North Americans, eating is about efficiency, not pleasure! I know, I know ... lucky me!

With love,
Mona

Sunday, September 29, 1991

Aba said he loves his shifts at the gas station and doesn't miss working at the bank at all!

"No more corner office with downtown views. No chai-wallah or snack-wallah to interrupt your concentration. And most importantly, no suit and tie! This uniform is a very distinct shade of lime green. It's wonderful," he extolled. The only problem that Tutoo and I can see is that the gas station is always open and he's always there, and Ami is even more cranky at home (if that's possible). But I'm still positive that this is all part of our adjustment period and then everything will sort itself out.

Monday, September 30, 1991

Today I thought a lot about that poem Hala told me about— the poem said that the deeper your loss, the greater the joy you will one day carry. I understand the poem a little better now, I think. Today I'm being visited by sorrow and my cup is empty and dry, but tomorrow it'll overflow with joy, right?

For sure, Waleed hurt me and disappointed me, but he also taught me something priceless—how deeply I *did* and *can* love.

Eulogy for Waleed by Mona Hasan, 11¾
Thoughts of you
Make the sky breezy, bright blue.
The sky is so beautifully blue
Blindingly bright blue
Because of thoughts of you.
Oh, what a great hue.
Thank you.

CHAPTER TEN

October

Tuesday, October 1, 1991

Day seven of regular Canadian school . . . and I *still* haven't had a conversation with a human my age! I thought everyone would approach me and pepper me with questions—I thought being a new and exotic student would inspire *some* curiosity from others! Not how it seems to work here. Everyone is just silently staring at me from a distance instead. Aren't they *at all* curious to get to know me? I was going to make up wild stories about my life in Dubai, like riding camels to school and being caught in sandstorms, and my father having a fleet of Lamborghinis. Alas, no one wants to hear any of my outlandish tales!

Wednesday, October 2, 1991

The strange thing is that our parents were so sure our lives would be better in Canada. Aba's no stranger to hard work—he's been a "workaholic" all his life, but there were always leisurely outings to the beach, at the very least. In Canada, the gas station stays open seven out of seven days, and Aba's shifts either begin at five in the evening or at midnight. We have *EVEN LESS* family time! The only way I can spend any quality time with my father is if I work at the gas station with him.

Thursday, October 3, 1991

It was in art class that my first interaction with a Canadian human my age *FINALLY* happened!! We reached for the same paint color—cerulean blue—but then we deferred to each other repeatedly until we both walked away with different tubes of paint. Right after class ended, he came up to my locker, where I was pretending I knew how to open it.

"You don't look like you're from around here. What are you? Like a halfie or something?"

"Halfie?"

"You know, Black dad, white mom. Sometimes the other way around, not often around here, but sometimes."

"No. I'm Pakistani. Well, kind of. My grandparents were actually from India but then India changed its name on all the maps."

"Huh?"

"Um, I was living in Dubai before I came here . . . the Middle East? You know. Oil. Camels. Bombs."

"Well, I'll be. You could pass, you know."

"Pass?"

"For a halfie."

"Uh, thank you?"

"Definitely. Halfies are, like, hot. I've seen your little sister in your mom's car trailing you home every afternoon. How come your sister's a whole other shade? And how come you don't get in the car with them?"

"They're so embarrassing, don't you think? And do you really think she's a whole other shade?"

"Is there a family anywhere that isn't embarrassing? Plus, it's so obvi—she's so much lighter than you."

"Well, I'll be."

"Yeah. Does she have a different dad?"

"No!"

"You guys don't look alike at all."

"We're sisters."

"There's a story there. Talk to your mom."

"You're ridiculous."

"No, I'm Ross. Hi."

"I'm Mona. Hello."

Ross says the most ridiculous and outrageous things—anything that pops into his head. There is zero filter between his brain and his mouth, and I just know that we're going to be great friends. We've made plans to meet for lunch tomorrow!

Friday, October 4, 1991

Ross is a boy but everyone thinks he's a girl. Maybe it's because of how he talks. Everyone speaks in black-and-white, but Ross speaks in colors. He's laugh-out-loud, piss-in-your-pants funny. And he moved here from Newfoundland last year, so he's new here—a Come From Away, just like me!

He taught me all the swear words he knows, and I taught him all the swear words I know. He said the Urdu and Arabic words in his Newfie accent, and I said the English and French words in my Pakistani-via-Dubai accent, and we spent the entire lunchtime snorting up our milk and I may or may not have wet my pants.

Saturday, October 5, 1991

I spent Saturday evening with Aba at the gas station. The time together was wonderful. He asked me all about school, and I told him all about the interesting, new things I've learned from my library books, like:

1. Who would have known it but every single person in Dartmouth came here as an immigrant too. Their grandparents or their great-grandparents or their great-great-grandparents came from such faraway places, like Scotland or Ireland or Britain or France or some interesting mix of those

countries! Well, except the Mi'kmaq—they are a people who were always here, even if all the history books start with when the immigrants from Europe arrived. What I don't get is that since the Mi'kmaq were here first, where are they now? We don't have a single person from the Mi'kmaq nation in our school, so I'm not at all sure how I will ever learn their swear words!

2. Many of the Black immigrants in Nova Scotia came as refugees after the American Revolution. That was some two hundred years ago! A hundred years ago, they made their own ice hockey league. But they were pushed off to live in neighborhoods without running water or paved roads or electricity. Neighborhoods named Africville, Cherry Brook and North Preston.

3. The largest human-made explosion in Nova Scotia was the Halifax Explosion. Two ships collided with each other and two thousand people died. I told Aba not to worry though, as this happened back in 1917 and explosions and chaos haven't happened here since then. I told him that he's chosen a really safe place for his family, and since we're neither Mi'kmaq nor Black, we should be okay. Besides, injustice against some people doesn't mean injustice against all, or does it?

Monday, October 7, 1991

Start of a new school week and I'm SO excited now that I have a friend at school. A FRIEND! A FRIEND! A REAL, PROPER FRIEND AND NOT ONE FROM A BOOK! Move aside, Anne of Green Gables. Make way for Ross of Dartmouth!

Today Ross and I met for lunch inside the art room. We talked about favorite paintings and artists. He complained about being stuck in the wrong town at the wrong time. "It's too small a town and it's too small a time. Big-city kids get to have all the fun. Small-town Canada can suck it. Instead of being the most popular kid here, I'm the pariah."

Why would anyone not want to be friends with Ross? He is the most fascinating person I've ever met.

Tuesday, October 8, 1991

The art room is Ross's sanctuary. "I can be my full, free, fabulous self only in a room with blank paper and tins of paint. Oh, the possibilities in front of us, Mona, when the canvas is blank!"

Wednesday, October 9, 1991

I found out today that blank pages are not the only reason Ross likes to have lunch in the art room. The art room is also a great hiding spot.

From bullies.

Jamie, an angry burly kid who sits in the back of my science class, was waiting outside the door for us to come out. So, actually, I guess, it wasn't such a great hiding spot after all.

When Ross opened the door, Jamie flicked his science textbook out of his arms. It splayed upside down on the hallway floor. The pages fanned out and were crushed together in sad folds. Jamie gave Ross a series of punches on each shoulder. He was laughing. And so was Ross. Ross laughed along even though the punches clearly hurt and even though he should have pushed back, given Jamie a good one to the gut, shouted NO. But Ross didn't. He continued smiling timidly. Meekly. Pathetically.

Then Jamie nailed Ross hard, a solid one in the stomach. Ross folded, gasped, then slowly straightened up again. Looked up at Jamie with eyes tearing up from the pain. "Heh, heh, yeah ... good one, yeah," Ross said, cuddling his left kidney and smiling.

I'm no fool. I knew there was no way Jamie would hit a girl, especially one with a headscarf, so I moved in front of Ross. Jamie made a big show of curtsying. "Ah, of course. Your *bodyguard*," he taunted, and then Jamie skedaddled out of the hallway quickly lest someone witness him having a conversation with me.

Thursday, October 10, 1991

"Hey, Ross. You play any sports?"

"..."

"Footsie-tootsie? Pansy-ball?"

Snicker. Snicker.

At the end of lunchtime, Jamie slammed Ross's shoulders against the lockers, then sprinted down the hallway. Ross kept his eyes on the floor the whole time.

I don't understand why he doesn't fight back.

Friday, October 11, 1991

Jamie and two of his sidekicks came by during afternoon recess. Ross kept his eyes on the floor. "How's it going, Rossy-Wossy? Hey, you have something on your shirt." Ross stayed still. Pretty much stopped breathing. "It's right there. You see it?" Jamie pressed a finger against Ross's chest, hard enough to make Ross stumble back. There was something on Ross's shirt after all. Jamie's finger had red paint on it. "You've been marked. Bull's-eye." Then Jamie walked off with his goons trailing after him.

Ross didn't stand up for himself. But worse than this, *I* didn't stand up for *him*.

Saturday, October 12, 1991

It's Saturday, so I'm at the gas station with Aba again.

What I've learned this week at school is that if you're different in any way in a Canadian public school, then one of two things is going to happen: Either you're going to be in a group called the Invisibles, or you're going to be in a group called the Targets.

I'm one of the Invisibles at school. Us Invisibles—we're kinda lucky, I guess. No one wants to bully us, *but* no one wants to talk to us either. Ross is one of the Targets—anyone in that group, they get picked on. "We'll stay in these groups for the rest of our lives," Ross told me miserably yesterday. He sighed and snapped his fingers. "Life isn't a Disney movie, Mona. You can't change your destiny just like that." Then the bell that signaled lunchtime was over rang loudly.

I thought about these groups while at the gas station, but I didn't know the words to talk to Aba about this, so I stayed quiet. Aba wasn't much in the mood for talking anyway. He had asked me to double-check some tax calculations for him, then got into a bad mood about how much tax he has to pay. We sat inside the gas station being surly together and mulling over our problems silently.

Sunday, October 13, 1991

School is closed tomorrow—it's for a North American festival called Thanksgiving. Families are supposed to gather and enjoy a meal together. The only family we have in this country is Uncle Ali and he's all the way in Toronto. In any case,

we can't really get everyone together for an evening meal—
the gas station has to stay open seven out of seven days.

Monday, October 14, 1991

All the Nova Scotian families, with aunts and uncles and
grandparents and cousins, are having yummy dinners together
tonight.

Here at home, we had a disastrous evening. Ami burned
two rotis. Tutoo complained about the smell of onions and
curry. Aba was at work all day.

I give thanks for nothing.

Tuesday, October 15, 1991

If Jamie wasn't a bully, I might even have had a crush on
him. He's got a cute face. There are dimples on both cheeks.
Big open smile. He looks like the type of kid smiling up at
you from a WELCOME TO CANADA poster. Harmless.
Friendly. You can't tell there's anything wrong with him just
by looking at him. He's not missing an arm or a leg. No patch
over an eye. No hooked hand. How did he end up such a
horrid bully?

Ross and I think that maybe his father wanted a girl. Or
maybe his mom ran off with the milkman. Or maybe Jamie's
puppy died a slow, painful death in his arms when he was five
and he's been embittered since then. Or for sure someone

stole all his Christmas presents one year. Maybe his One True Love stabbed him in the back and ran off with his nemesis or something terrible like that.

We've all got stories and excuses to be horrid to others, don't we, Allah?

Wednesday, October 16, 1991

Everyone's favorite teacher is Mr. D. He's the English teacher. His classroom is peppered with inspirational quotes, and he's basically read every book under the sun. In his class, the students pay extra attention. I know this because the girls sit up with breasts pointing out and the boys even pull up their pants.

He's hosting a poetry competition—any poem, any length, on any theme! The winning poem will be the one that "moves" him most. Well, if he wants to move, then I'll make mine extra snazzy and rhyming! The submissions are due on a day called Halloween.

Thursday, October 17, 1991

Ross has invited me over to his house after school tomorrow so we can work on our poetry submissions for Mr. D.'s contest! Ross wants to do a poem about a little boy who gets lost in a flower garden, falls asleep under a tree and wakes up with wings. But if Jamie gets a copy of the poem, he's sure to pick on Ross even more, so while Ross is going to write his poem, he won't submit it. Which sucks for him as his voice goes unheard but is perfectly fine for me as it's less competition! I haven't decided what to write my poem on, but since all the great poets seem to wax lyrical about the joys of nature, I'll likely write an ode to the magnificent mango.

The most exciting thing is having a playdate at Ross's home! Tutoo's been to Sofia Rousopoulos's place for hundreds of playdates already, and now it's finally my turn to go to a friend's!

After lying down dead for an hour, I finally got my parents to agree to let me walk to Ross's home with him after school! I wonder what his home is like inside? I'm guessing super clean and super expensive. I better be careful not to break anything!

Friday, October 18, 1991

We had to walk over an old moldy aquarium left at the front entrance.

Ross has three younger sisters and a loud mother. His mother immediately started yelling at him when she saw me. "You brought a friend home? Another girl? When are you going to bring back someone you can pass a puck around with? Go on a muddy bike ride? Play some violent video game? What are you two going to do—cross-stitch some butterflies? Ice some cupcakes? Stick flowers in your hair? *Gahwd*."

Ross muttered, "Shut it, you ole windpipe," under his breath and we went upstairs to take refuge in his bedroom.

Ross told me about all the pressure he feels at home being the only boy in the family, and the pressure he feels at school being so different from the other boys. All this time, I thought being a girl was difficult. Girls have to be pretty but shouldn't know it. Smart but not smart*er*. Friendly but not *slutty*. Meanwhile boys have it rough too. They have to be smart but not nerdy. Sporty but not short. Confident but not cocky. If they like baking or ribbons or catchy pop songs, then they have to keep it to themselves, otherwise someone's going to punch them in the face at school. They're supposed to *like* girls but not *be like* girls. It sounds dead confusing and arduous, and the once-a-month shark attack in my yooha seems like a fair trade-off now.

The other thing Ross and I talked about is that his mother's been diagnosed with bipolar disorder. "It's no big deal," he said, but he also told me how he's called the cops on her three times in the past two years.

"What can the police do when she's in one of her moods?" I asked.

"Nothing, really, but when she sees the cop car come careening down the street, flashers on, it calms her down somehow. The more the shit hits the fan, the more relaxed she becomes. And she remembers, 'Oh yeah, have to take me pills.'"

He shrugged.

He shared his truths so easily and so openly that I wanted to know how freeing that would feel. Friendship is pulling your heart out of your chest and offering it to someone, isn't it? You risk it being squashed, or comforted.

Before leaving I shared two of my important truths with Ross—one, that my mother's been in and out of naps since her pregnancy, and that truth be told, it's gotten worse since moving to Canada. I told Ross that she's been having a hard time adjusting. Adapting. I complained that she naps all the time. Since coming to Canada, I hadn't seen her *not* in a sleeping position in what felt like years.

"Depression," he said.

"There's a word for it?" I asked, awestruck.

"Sure, Mona. There's a word for EVERYTHING."

I wonder if knowing the right word for what's happening in your world means that you can change your destiny, Allah. Secondly, I told Ross that as per polite Pakistani guest etiquette, I was *supposed* to refuse his first two offers of food or drink, and that as per gracious host etiquette, *he* was *supposed* to offer *at least* three times. "For the love of Allah, feed me," I told him, my stomach rumbling. "If I go home hungry, my parents will never let me come back here again." Ross laughed and hurriedly ran to heat up food in the kitchen. I snarfed down the most delicious North American cuisine I've had yet—Hot Pockets!

Saturday, October 19, 1991

Sam walked into the gas station with his father today, but he pretended he didn't know me. Our fathers introduced themselves, then Sam's father introduced his son to me: "You two must be in same school." We nodded nonchalantly, as if this was the most boring information in the universe. Sam's father told my father how he came to Canada decades ago from his birth country and that his son Sam was born here—"My son, no accent." He jabbed a finger at Sam's chest, and shrugged like the no-accent thing was no big deal. Then he puffed up his chest and the buttons on his shirt almost popped off. How lucky and brilliant was he to have had the foresight to abandon his birth country so long ago! How unfortunate and pathetic were we to have hoped against the odds for longer.

My father straightened his back and arched his thumb toward me. "My daughter, fluent in her mother tongue and yours too." I shrank at my father's bald-faced lie. No way did my father think my Urdu and Arabic were anywhere as good as they should be, so I closed my eyes and hoped that no one would quiz me on my mother tongue or their own. Sam's father cleared his throat. He placed his keychain on the counter. Clearly he drove a very fancy car, and my father had to admit defeat.

Our fathers moved on from the volatile topics of their income levels and the integration of their children into mainstream Canadian society into safer topics like Middle Eastern dictatorships. As they threw themselves into politics,

Sam hissed, "Nice pants," at me. I looked down at my sequined jeans from Value Village. They *were* nice—I had spent an entire hour looking for pants like these. Not only did I find sequined denim pants, but they were also pleated! Sequined *and* pleated jeans were a big thing in the fashion magazines Laila and I would look at back home, but I knew instantly from Sam's tone that they weren't fashionable here.

I changed topics. "Do you know how to write your name in Arabic?"

He shook his head no.

I smiled sweetly and flattened a roll of receipt paper. I took him off to the side and showed him how to trace the words going from right to left. I watched serenely as he wrote "I am a donkey" over and over.

Sunday, October 20, 1991

Aba walked into my bedroom this morning carrying something he had found in the bottom of my backpack last night.

"Mona, we need to talk. I know home life right now is not the best. These are trying times for us. Your mother. Her hormones. But we need to stay strong. Oh Allah, I must just come out and ask it. How long you are doing drugs, beta? I found this in your backpack. Oh Allah, where did I go wrong? What have I done?"

"Uff, *Aba!*"

"Oh, Allah!"

"Stop it, Aba! It's not a joint, it's a tampon. You even sell these at your store . . ."

"Tam? Pon? Listen, whatever they call it these days, I don't want you becoming a druggie. Did I throw away my promotion at the Dubai bank for *this*?"

"This is the worst day *EVER* . . ."

"You keep smoking this thing and you'll be on the streets—homeless. Hungry. Hurt. We could have just married you off in Pakistan then . . ."

"Aba, please stop talking. It's not for drugs. It's a girl thing. We use it in the washroom. Don't worry about it and please don't touch my things. This is the grossest day of my life."

"Girl thing? Washroom? Well. Of course, of course. Have you talked to your mother about this *tam-pon sham-pon*?"

"Aba, she's always sleeping."

"She's too delicate for this world. Are you helping out enough in the kitchen?"

"Are you?"

"Me? I'm a man. Don't be ridiculous, Mona."

He accused *me* of being ridiculous? Isn't it *this* world, that *You've* created, that is completely ridiculous?

Monday, October 21, 1991

Since this world is so ridiculous, I did something ridiculous.

I'm one of the Invisibles, right? I can do what I want. The whole walk to school, no one batted an eyelid. At school, no one walking down the hallway did a double-take. None of the teachers blinked twice either. Ross was the only one who noticed by claiming he didn't notice. He came up to me during a class change.

"There's something different about you, Mona. I can't quite put my finger on it."

"*ROSS!!!*"

"Mascara? You've got mascara on?!"

"Come on. I know you know. I don't believe this."

"Your mother's lipstick maybe? Some shiny lip gloss, isn't it?"

"Ross! *Obviously* you know. My headscarf, Ross. It's off."

"Well, I'll be."

"Come on, give it to me. What do you think?"

"Well, the dandruff . . ."

"*ROSS!!*"

"The best parts of you are everything my eyes can't see, okay? Keep it on or take it off. A piece of cloth on your head doesn't change you to me."

Why'd I decide to take it off, Allah? For the same reason I put it on, of course—I *wanted* to.

And if I want to put it back on again, maybe because of another bad haircut, or because it makes me feel closer to You or to this past summer, or maybe because I know it will rile up my Dadi, or remind me of who I was and where I came from and will make the path ahead more comforting and less unfamiliar and scary, then I'll put it back on again and the decisions I make about the clothes on my body won't be anyone else's but mine, will they, Allah?

Tuesday, October 22, 1991

Aba insisted on dropping me off at school today and subjected me to one of his inspirational father-daughter talks.

"Mona, you know the best inventions we have are because of someone making mistakes?"

"Huh?"

"Progress. Progress. Uffo, I'm talking about progress, Mona. Wake up. This thing called progress, it only happens because someone tried. We have improvement only because of failed experiments."

"Okay, Aba."

"I'm saying you must *TRY*. There is no shame in the *TRY*. Go up to someone. Join a club. Reach out and say hello."

"I have a friend, Aba. I'm fine."

"So why you look so miserable every day?"

"It's my face, Aba."

"Fix it."

I had never noticed how strange my father is. He seemed normal in Dubai, but it's quite clear that he has become terribly, utterly weird. And by *weird*, I mean he's a PLANET-SIZED BAZONGO ball of weirdness. I am certain that he is the one who has changed and not me.

Wednesday, October 23, 1991

It wasn't an ode to the mango, but a poem came tumbling out late last night. It's personal and different but it feels important, so I'm going to work on it and polish it and send it in for Mr. D.'s poetry competition.

The one thing that seems certain is that the best way to set myself up to win is to be fearless about failing. To try out as many drafts as possible. Write. Rewrite. Revise. Toss. Delete.

Fail.

Start again.

Again and again until the piece of paper *soars*.

There's only one way to get better, right? With my heart throbbing its way up my throat and sweat pouring down my face. Whether it's a poem or sport or love or Capital *L* Life, if I'm going up to bat for something, then the only way I'm doing it is by giving it everything I've got.

Thursday, October 24, 1991

Worked on my poem all night. Wrote and rewrote. Then this morning, I handwrote it neatly and slid it into Mr. D.'s submission box at the front of the class. FINGERS CROSSED (except for that troublesome middle finger).

Friday, October 25, 1991

The one nice thing about being in Canada is that my family finally realizes how important I am.

Aba takes me to the bank with him and pushes me to the front so I do all the talking with the bank-wallahs. It's important practice, he tells me. Ami's always tired so she asks me to fill out all the school forms, and I'm even allowed to sign the permission slips! Tutoo runs all her homework by me, and asks me questions on Canadian history and geography and custom and traditions. Being a spokesperson for my family has made me *even better* at making up lies on the spot.

Saturday, October 26, 1991

At the store Aba rocked back and forth on his heels.

"I have come up with genius great idea. Do you want to know?"

I nodded politely.

He pulled a large cardboard box from the back room. Slid it in front of me. The box came up to my waist.

"Your birthday it is coming up, right? We need sales to go up at store, right? This was fifty percent off, right? Do you get it? Open it and you'll get it."

I opened the box slowly. I was scared.

I pulled out stiff red tights with three large red toes meant to go over shoes. A fuzzy yellow body followed. A large yellow head with a red comb and a wobbly red wattle. Orange beak.

227

"Are you getting it now? Canadians—they are loving animals, right? This is the mighty chicken! You stand at the corner of Woodlawn and Main. Flap the chicken wings and entice customers to come in for gas. Sales will go up fatafat fast. I came to this country for your future and Tutoo's future only. The one thing you can do for your poor, sacrificing father is that you can put this chicken suit on, do small chicken dance and get more bloody customers in here."

Sunday, October 27, 1991

Little kids wanted to pull on the wattle. A few bigger small kids pulled on my short tail. Two mothers wanted me to pose for pictures with their children. Otherwise I counted my blessings that no one could see it was me inside.

At one point, it seemed like Sam and his father drove by, but I'm not entirely sure, so I'm going to pretend that it wasn't them.

Monday, October 28, 1991

Sam was walking down the hallway holding hands with Keesha Beals today. She's only the school's most popular and pretty girl. I thought I heard "cluck, cluck" from somewhere behind me.

I made Ross take a sharp U-turn in the hallway.

Tuesday, October 29, 1991

No Sam sighting today.

What does a perfect girl like Keesha Beals see in a toad like Sam?

Wednesday, October 30, 1991

Important Candy and Chocolate Festival tomorrow!

Canadians will give out mithai for free tomorrow evening! You just have to knock on their doors and the polite Canadians throw the candy *they* paid for into *your* pillowcases and wish you a very good night!

Daft Canadians! (But at least sales at the gas station were up.)

Thursday, October 31, 1991

Tutoo was so excited by the thought of free candy and chocolate that she got up at 5:00 a.m.!! She even made her own costume last night by turning a brown yard-waste bag upside down and cutting out neck- and arm-holes. Then she made a crown with yellow felt and an old headband. She wrote "PRINCESS" in black Sharpie on the front of the bag and slipped it over a long-sleeved black shirt and black tights. The "Paper Bag Princess" is a character from a famous Canadian book. Tutoo put a lot of thought and time into her costume.

I didn't.

I put on the chicken suit.

Also, totally overlooked by everyone but it was my birthday today. To be honest, even I was surprised how suddenly my birthday arrived! I usually do a two-week countdown, but I've been distracted by all the new things in my life, and I guess so have the rest of my family.

After school we stood around a store-bought cake that Ami wrangled out of a plastic box with a "HALF OFF" sticker on the side. My family sang a halfhearted "Happy Birthday." Tutoo inhaled her piece of cake, whined until I hurriedly put on my chicken suit costume and then dragged me out into the blustery October evening for the candy-collecting fun.

The only good thing about today was discovering that the leaves actually do turn yellow. Golden, in fact.

Happy birthday to me.
Happy birthday to me.
I look like a wombat and feel like its poo.
Happy birthday to me.

Are all my birthdays in Canada going to be this miserable, Allah?

CHAPTER ELEVEN

November

Friday, November 1, 1991

Last night, Aba refused to participate in the candy festival. He said he wasn't going to give out free candy if anyone knocked. "I am already paying too much in taxes," he grumbled and turned off all the lights.

Saturday, November 2, 1991

Good news is that the weather has turned chillier, so Ami made Aba retire the chicken costume.

Sunday, November 3, 1991

Bad news is that this meant that I had to spend time with Aba inside the gas station. As I was held captive, Aba asked me—

"Did you know that several types of octopuses have blue blood? Did you know that the giant Pacific octopus has three hearts and nine brains? Did you know this? What do they teach you at school?"

I missed the chicken costume.

Monday, November 4, 1991

Mr. D. asked to talk to me in private tomorrow!! Could this have something to do with the poem I submitted for the class contest?!! ~~Maybe~~ Of course, it does! He's going to tell me that I've won! My itty-bitty heart is swollen with pride! I will also use this as an opportunity to tell Mr. D. about the bullying that's happening to Ross. He's one of the best teachers here. He'll be able to help—I'm sure of it.

Tuesday, November 5, 1991

Mr. D. kept me after class to accuse me of cheating.

Staying longer cut into my lunchtime, but I thought he was going to congratulate me on winning the top prize in the poetry contest, so I was happy to. Instead he asked me a series of questions suspiciously—

"You just moved to Canada?"

"Yes."

"And where did you move from?"

"Dubai."

"And where is that again?"

"In the United Arab Emirates."

". . ."

"Next to Saudi Arabia."

"Yes, yes. I know that region well."

"Uh, yes."

"So you're an Aye-rub?"

"Arab? Um, no."

"But you speak Aye-rub?"

"*Arabic*? A little, yes."

"And you were living in the United States of Aye-rubs?"

"Emirates. United Arab *Emirates*. Um, okay, yes, I was."

"Your poem was good."

"Oh, thank you."

"*Very* good . . ."

"Oh gee, thank you so very . . ."

"*Too* good. In *this* country, cheating is a serious crime. We don't copy other people's work and pass it off as our own. It's called *play-jah-reez-sum*, and you can get into serious trouble for it here. In *my* country, we take pride in doing our *own* work *ourselves*. We have *big* computers that check for this kind of stuff. Come back tomorrow and tell me where you got this poem from. I wasn't born yesterday. You can't even look me in the eye, you barely speak any English, and you just moved here from the United States of Aye-rubs."

When I came back from school, I told the parents what Mr. D. had said.

During the telling, Aba's and Ami's eyes widened to bursting, then narrowed to slits, then widened again. At the end of my retelling, they looked at each other, puffed up their chests and smiled proudly! "To be accused of cheating means that you are ahead of your class fellows by kilometers! This is a great compliment to you. To *us*," Aba said.

Ami livened up enough to come to a sitting position on the futon. "You know, two great-aunts on my side dabbled in poetry too."

"No teacher has ever accused *me* of cheating," Tutoo wailed and sulked off to the bedroom.

Aba said to leave the conversation about where the poem came from to him. "I'll call Mr. D. and the principal tomorrow and thank them for such a *special* compliment."

Wednesday, November 6, 1991

Last night, Ami and Aba were talking about Mr. D. Aba said he felt embarrassed and humiliated having to take in my report cards to show my teacher that I was capable. He bemoaned that Mr. D. continued to disbelieve that I was completing my assignments without cheating.

Aba paced the living room floor while Ami remained horizontal on the futon. They stayed up late speaking in Urdu with many swear words.

They spoke about lines drawn sharp and straight, or sometimes squiggled rough and jagged, on maps and atlases. Lines that separated grandparents from grandchildren. Their voices rose as they discussed the money and machinery spent on partition and borders and walls, and how ordinary families spent their lives fighting and resisting, fleeing and hiding, and how tiring it was to undo all the divisions and try to find, and multiply into, big colorful families again.

"It will not do. It will not do." Aba stomped and ranted. "They make it so you have to leave and when you get where they wanted you gone, they make it so you long to head back."

Maybe it was because the baby in Ami's stomach stirred but at some point, the anger rolled and their voices softened. Their tones shifted. "Maybe the winds will blow, maybe things will change." *Maybe this. Maybe that.* They joked that maybe Aba should run for office. "Heather Hasan for prime minister!" they said and laughed in hushed howls, thinking we were asleep. They laughed until they said it hurt, it hurt very much. Then they stayed quiet for a while so that when it happened, I heard it very clearly.

Aba, who has never prayed, went to the linen closet to get the prayer rug we keep for guests. I heard the closet door creak open. The fabric unfurled and was spread in a corner of the living room. I heard the Allahu Akbars, and I heard

235

Aba's forehead on the floor. Ami softly pulled the covers over her head and resumed her twenty-hour nap. After finishing his prayers, Aba changed into his uniform for the closing shift, rounded his shoulders and headed out into the cold, black sky.

Where do you take the love that is not wanted, Allah? The heart aches to lay it down somewhere, doesn't it?

Thursday, November 7, 1991

I was wrong about Mr. D. He's only popular with the popular kids. The Invisibles and the Targets don't like him too much. Also, he clearly hasn't read all the books in the world. He's only read the books in *his* world. What I mean is that what he thinks about me, and what I can or cannot do, has nothing to do with me. It has to do with him, with what he knows and what he doesn't know. It does suck that he thinks so poorly of me, and it's not something I'm used to, and I hope I never do get used to such a feeling! Anyway, *no time to mope. Must plant hope.*

Sure, I can sit around and mope and feel sorry about myself for what Mr. D. said, or I can focus on something much more important—my friend Ross. I don't want him to be bullied anymore—*You have to reach out and grab the life you want.*

I have to figure something out.

Friday, November 8, 1991

Working at the gas station with Aba has taught me that there are two kinds of customers in the world.

Man. Woman. Old. Young. Doesn't matter. Two kinds of customers in this world: Patrons either believe that it's enough to pay for their snacks and gas with money, or they believe that kindness is important too. Half the customers throw their change on the counter and walk out, and the other half make eye contact, smile and nod "thank you."

Saturday, November 9, 1991

Aba and I listened to a sports reporter on the radio recap how the Chicago Bulls won four games over the L.A. Lakers this summer. At the end of the highlight reel, Aba stroked his chin. "Never should underestimate an underdog," Aba mused. "Sometimes the person who has the least chance of winning can swoop in last minute and fatafat fast take the top spot." His comments were a welcome change from tedious facts on marine animals, but I wondered what was really on his mind. Then he turned around and tenderly wiped the dust off the frames of his degrees, which were hanging lopsided on the wall behind the cash register.

"Do you feel like you're an underdog in Canada?" I asked Aba gingerly.

Aba snorted.

"Mona, I'm being lucky if I was underdog. No. I'm the dirt under the dog. But you, *you* get to be underdog. You marry correctly and study properly like I tell you, then your children can be regular dogs."

Monday, November 11, 1991

Remembrance Day. School closed.

Canada has this holiday because on the eleventh hour of the eleventh day of the eleventh month, World War I came to an end.

Why do schools only teach us about the wars that are over? And not the ones happening right now?

Tuesday, November 12, 1991

Substitute teacher in science class today. A Mr. Patel. Everyone in class copied his accent behind his back and tittered. At first I didn't get it, but then I guess I got it? He sounded like the country he's from, which was India of course, and that was . . . *funny*? Ha, I guess. I mean, it's a running joke on that cartoon with yellow people and blue hair on TV, so I supposed it did make sense. But actually I was confused. Then Jamie, slouched in the back row, bellowed to Mr. Patel, "Hey, Mr. P. Give us your signature catchphrase, why dontcha?"

Mr. Patel looked confused but smiled shyly. "Oh, you children. That's enough, now. Focus, everyone. Focus." Then the class really erupted into guffaws. Mr. Patel didn't get it. Why would he?

He didn't know that his accent emphasized the first half of the word in a most unfortunate manner. *Foc*-us, indeed.

As the class hyena-ed themselves crazy, Keesha Beals (yes, yes, only the school's prettiest and most popular girl, as You well know, Allah—the princess to the toad that is Sam) whipped around from the front row and stared at me as I tried to shrink into a speck in my seat. "Hey, you— Moon-a. Is Mr. Patel from the same country as you?" she shrilled loudly.

Is he? Isn't he? I mean, technically yes. Or is it technically no? Yes. No. I don't know. In that pregnant pause while Keesha stared and waited for my answer, I knew that if I answered no, it would be because I was ashamed of where he's from, and ultimately where I'm from, and this would cause grief to my beloved Dadi across the world and shame inside me, and really I was much too young to die of shame (and much too pretty too).

"Hmm, yes, same-same," I mumbled, head down, speaking into my chest. Maybe Keesha wouldn't hear what I said?

Oh, but Keesha heard all right.

What she did next was something I didn't expect. Something I didn't even have the audacity to imagine. She straightened her back. Spoke loudly and crisply to the class in general but one person in particular. "Knock it off. Don't be such a disgrace. I know you can do better."

The tittering stopped abruptly and there was pin-drop silence for a full ten seconds. Then some shuffling and sheepish looks, and a few kids mumbled, "I didn't think it was funny either." Jamie adjusted the baseball cap on his head and slunk down in his seat. He didn't speak again for the rest of the class.

Ya Allah, how breathtaking and spectacular it is that Anne with an E was right. That, in fact, this world is abundant in "kindred spirits" after all, and we need only to look around, reach out and find them.

Wednesday, November 13, 1991

I saw a blueprint for bravery yesterday and today I copied it.

Today when Jamie came up to Ross, I slid myself between them.

Some of the things I thought about saying—That's enough. Stop. Stop this. Stop and think. Stop now. You can be better than this. Why are you doing this? Why are you angry? What if someone was doing this to your younger brother? Your younger sister? Do you need help? You are better than this.

In the end, I pretty much copied Keesha Beals word-for-word—*I know you can do better*—and while I didn't quite stare him down (I mean, he's so much taller than me), I did *really* look at him. And I tell you, when you don't like someone, *really* looking into their eyes is uncomfortable business, for both of you.

Jamie blanched but he got it. "Was just havin' a bit of fun. Geez. Don't be so uptight, Moo-Ana. Sheesh." Jamie huffed and moved away. We didn't see him again for the rest of the day.

Thursday, November 14, 1991

Jamie hasn't so much as looked at Ross today.

"This is so unusual, and it feels so strange not to be picked on. I wonder if I should throw *myself* against the lockers today," quipped Ross at lunch.

"Now you're an Invisible too. Welcome to a new world," I quipped back.

In other news, I've decided I'm going to sign up for the grade seven girls' basketball team. Tryouts are this Saturday. The stats are that the team has lost every major game for the last nine years, so standards are low and they will accept castaways. Coach is our very own frazzled school secretary, Ms. McLean, who made a point of reminding everyone that she is not paid for her extracurricular coaching activities, so she expects to be compensated by our commitment and passion instead. Wish me luck!

Friday, November 15, 1991

Sherry Alfaro moved here from El Salvador a year ago. She's an Invisible too. Ross and I have seen her spend her lunchtimes alone at the library reading chapter books for younger kids.

As soon as the lunch bell rang today, we dashed over to tap her on the arm before she slid into the library. She's an ESL-Invisible, so we had to mime and ask her twice before she understood that we were wondering if she wanted to eat lunch with us. She was so startled that she snorted nervously. Then she said "si" quickly.

Sharing a lunch with someone is like sharing your insides. Opening a lunchbox is opening a door into your most real self. Sherry ate two small, round corn-cakes for lunch, which she told us are called pupusas. Ross had a Lunchables box, and I had my aloo parathas. We mixed and matched and traded and bemoaned our mothers, who refused to make us white bread sandwiches for school.

Today I learned that after "It's going to be okay," the five kindest words to say to anyone are "Wanna have lunch with me?"

With a lot of smiles and in broken English, Sherry answered all the crazy questions Ross and I had about her life in El Salvador. She escaped a civil war in her country. She told us that she and her brother dodged bullets by day and made a kids' newspaper by night. They called it *The Daily Blah* (*El Bla Diario*). They made up pretend letters from Salvadorans complaining about the price of sugar and tomatoes, and included riddles and jokes for their younger readers.

Sherry said she's seen some basketball on TV, so I've asked her to come to the tryouts tomorrow. Wish us luck!

Saturday, November 16, 1991

Tryouts consisted of running around the muddy field for two kilometers without pause. That was eleven loops.

Everyone who showed up and ran without passing out now has a spot on the team. Ms. McLean said that as long as we've got the WANT, she will teach the HOW. For basketball, you have to *want* something called *vertical*. Vertical means that you have to jump really high—that's how you can get the ball into the net. To jump high, you must first believe that you can fly. Coach ended the tryouts with a rousing speech: "Come on, lovies, I'll tell yah rate now the secret sauce for winnin' . . . yah must dust off yer self-pity. Look yahself in the mirror and ask yahself: One, is today the day I'm gonna believe in mahself or nah? Enn two, am I just gonna stay safe from risk 'n' disappointment 'n' warm a bench me whole life, or am I gon' spend my one life dyin' and tryin'? Tryin' and flyin' like I was born ter do?" Then she added, "Practices be twice a week now—Mondays and Thursdays. All games on Sundays. Be on time or donna bother."

How daft, right?

We can't *actually* fly, can we, Allah?

Sunday, November 17, 1991

I told Aba about the basketball tryouts yesterday and the practice after school tomorrow. He frowned. "How you going to manage so much, Mona? Work at gas station, make your grades A-one, help your mother with baby sister or brother soon. Now basketball too?"

"I'm an underdog, remember?"

Aba tilted his head to the side and shook it slowly. "Not so easy to be, Mona."

"Yeah, but I've got wings. You'll see."

Monday, November 18, 1991

At the practice after school, we played a "friendly" (which means that we were just playing among ourselves, with relaxed rules). "Zero-pressure game," Coach McLean called it. Sherry was pretty good on her feet and quick with the drills, so Coach McLean said she'd dust off the Spanish she knew from her college years.

As for the rest of us, Coach said, "It's quite-a clear that none of yah believe in yahselves or in flyin' . . . *yet*. Not ter worry. There be lots of time yet to turn yah sissies into believers."

Tuesday, November 19, 1991

I feel sorry for the kids born in Canada. None of them have a memory of their first time. To them, it's an ordinary thing.

It was in math class when it happened. I stared dumbly out the window. The other students all had their heads down, focused on their worksheets. How could they not marvel?

My knee bobbed up and down, and before I could stop myself, I sprang up from my seat and stood up by my desk. The chair scraped against the floor, and everyone turned to stare. I needed a better view of the cascading crystals on the other side of the window. On the walk home, it was only the younger kids and me who stuck our tongues out to taste this wondrous, magical manna from the heavens.

S-N-O-W!

Wednesday, November 20, 1991

This morning, I used the toe of my boot to dislodge some ice on the sidewalk. Then kicked it down the sidewalk, weaving between pedestrians until I reached school. By the afternoon, the wondrous snow turned from white cascading crystals to a sooty, slushy mess on the sidewalks and streets. No wonder no one gives it a second glance.

Thursday, November 21, 1991

Keesha Beals won the poetry contest. The poem was about her summer at her family's cottage. It was actually pretty good. Even if I didn't quite understand all of it, seeing as how I've never even been to whatever this thing called "cottage" is!

But I liked it. The cottage sounded peaceful. The lake was calm. The sky was pink and blue at sunset. The smell of her mother's raspberry and rhubarb pie was in the air, and the loons were calling (whatever they sound like).

Mr. D. passed around a new assignment today, which is due the first day after the winter break. Ugh! Another one already! I took the sheet of paper with the heading "Heroes in Our Community" and quickly stuffed it into my backpack. He said "heroism" is a theme we'll talk about next semester.

I'd better get started on this assignment early though. What I know for sure is that I definitely don't want to be accused of cheating again. After class, Mr. D. came up to me and cleared his throat noisily. Shifted from foot to foot. "Uh, um, yeah, so Mina, no cheating this time, okay. I gave you a pass on your last assignment, but I can't do that every time you have your daddy call in for you."

UGH. I didn't say anything back because it felt like I'd lost before even being given the chance to play.

But guess what: I'm going to show him!

Friday, November 22, 1991

NEW KID ALERT!

I will now be dethroned as New Kid and am ecstatic to pass the torch along!

New Kid's name is Adam. Dark hair, dark eyes. Olive skin.

He's moved here from the city of Calgary, which is in the province of Alberta, in the western part of Canada. He's super into sports and was wearing a Blue Jays cap. Better go catch up on hockey ASAP!

Saturday, November 23, 1991

At the gas station, I thought about how quickly Adam had been welcomed at John A. Macdonald Junior High. Yesterday was his first day but he's already made so many friends. Everyone went up to talk to him. They all had questions about his life in Calgary. What sports did he play? What's Stampede like? Has he been to Banff? Jasper? Seen a bear? What does he think of the Oilers?

What I noticed was that each time he smiled, the whole room lit up.

Sunday, November 24, 1991

I feel it deep in the recesses of my soul that Adam may be the puzzle piece to a mystery that I have been searching to solve all my life. Yes, he *is* the missing puzzle piece to my soul. *PUZZLE*. PIECE. TO. MY. SOUL!

Puzzle by Mona Hasan, 12
Oh, my missing piece of puzzle!
That I just want to nuzzle.

Oh, how I long for a tussle
With my puzzle!

Monday, November 25, 1991

Heard Adam's last name today. *Mr. Shah Peero*, someone down the hallway yelled and high-fived him. *Adam Shah Peero*.

The last name doesn't help me place him, country-wise. Not a very common Muslim name, actually. Downright unusual, in fact.

Where *is* he from?

Oh well.

The only thing I need to know right now is might he like me back? Does he, might he, could he, possibly in any small way, find me enticing? The rest is just details.

Shakespeare said that the course of true love never did run smooth. And so it is for Adam and me. I have heard through the grapevine that Keesha Beals is thinking of dumping Sam to ask Adam to the Winter Dance coming up next month! If she asks him, and if he says yes, then my life will be over.

What can I do, ya Allah? Asking him out on a date myself is out of the question. We have never had a conversation except the ones in my head and they don't count. I need a Sign from *You* that his heart belongs to *ME*!

Tuesday, November 26, 1991

On a silver chain, he was wearing a pendant with a six-pointed star on it!

!!!

!!!!!!!!!!!!!!!!!!!!!!!!!!!!!!

I *like* stars!

That's the Sign, isn't it?!

Wednesday, November 27, 1991

Well, I'm not waiting for Keesha Beals to walk off into the sunset with my Dreamboat, am I?! After math class yesterday, I took a deep breath and turned to Adam, walking out of the room for lunch, and said oh-so-casually, as if I'd just noticed it for the first time, "Cool pendant. I would love to know a little bit more about it . . ."

That's when I found out that it's not just *any* star. He explained that it's a Magen David, which is Hebrew for Star of David, and his bubbie, or grandmother, gifted it to him when he was seven. Which means that his last name's *Shapiro*, not *Shah Peero*, and that he's Jewish. Which means we're still having ten babies and being together until the end of time.

I asked more questions about where he's from and where his grandparents came from. He spoke about what they endured. How they survived. How they pivoted to thrive. It was fascinating stuff. "You really don't know any of this history?" he asked, fascinated.

I tried to explain that in Dubai it took a lot of work to unearth certain stories. That there were brave distributors like Hala and that there were plenty of brave readers too, but I questioned him if it wasn't the same thing here—weren't certain stories and voices buried here too? He nodded silently, frowning. Clearly I had disturbed him, and I wasn't happy to see him upset, but what I could also tell is that he was interested in what I was saying, and that swirl of curiosity and compassion in his eyes made my heart soar. "It seems like we both have a lot of catching up to do," he said and smiled. We agreed to exchange our favorite books by writers from faraway places. I can't wait!

Thursday, November 28, 1991

WORST day EVER.

I may crawl into bed and never get out again.

"Flag Football" at gym today.

Mr. Barry picked the two loudest kids to be captains, who in turn picked kid after kid in a long, drawn-out, embarrassing leave-the-loser-for-the-last torture-fest.

Why, oh why, couldn't Mr. Barry pick the Invisibles to be the captains? Both teams grumbled about who should get stuck with *ME* in front of *ME*! But, ya Allah, this wasn't even the worst of it.

Out on the field, everything was going fine until someone threw that stupid cone-shaped ball right at me, and by sheer stupidity and misfortune, I caught it! I cradled it under my left armpit and ran for my life before the hordes of pork-fed, eight-footed demons trampled me to death. I made it into the white gates of the goalpost, and half the demon hordes started yelling, "Touchdown! Touchdown!" I just stood there stunned and unsure until someone shouted, "Touch the %$&*^! ball down onto the ground, Has-Anne!" So I laid the ball carefully on the grass. Half the pork-fed hordes cheered and whooped loudly enough to cause me permanent ear damage, and the other half (which happened to be the half on my team) groaned. Of course! *Of course* I was on the wrong side! I had laid the ball down on my *own* team's goalpost! The bell rang and I shuffled back to the locker room.

Friday, November 29, 1991

BEST DAY EVER!!

Adam walked by as I was fidgeting with my locker and said, "Hey, Mona. Impressive sprint. Just figure out which direction you need to go next time." He patted me on the left shoulder and walked off. I know I didn't imagine it because Sherry and Ross saw the *WHOLE* thing and came sashaying over after Adam left so we could dissect the interaction in minute detail.

All I know is that the shirt I was wearing when he touched my shoulder will never see the light of day again! It's going under my pillow.

Saturday, November 30, 1991

I can*NOT* believe what happened today!

I was working the closing shift with Aba at the gas station. We were both behind the cash register, stuffing dimes and nickels into cardboard coin roll tubes, when I heard the jingle of bells from the front door. LO AND BEHOLD—it was Adam Shapiro pushing through the glass door and entering the store!!!

I immediately lost all control of my body. Behind the counter, my hands started to shake. Sweat drenched my armpits. My shoulders rounded. My neck folded into my chest. My eyes darted from speck to speck on the floor. Alas, the floor did not open up and welcome me. I was still there. In my father's store. Solidly in human form. With Adam Shapiro having just walked in. I began to blush. Unfortunately my actions did not go unnoticed by my father, the intrepid connoisseur of animal psychology. Before I could do anything, my father beckoned Adam over.

"Young boy, what is your name being?"

"Um, hi, sir. My name is Adam Shapiro."

"You are knowing my daughter? Look, this is my daughter. My daughter Mona Hasan. She is blushing. For sure, she is knowing you. You go to same school?"

"Yes, sir, we're both in the same math class together. Gym too."

"Wonderful, wonderful. Math. And gym. Top class subjects. She is A-one in math, you know. Soon she will be top in gym too. She is growing wings, you know." *Stop. Stop. Just stop.* I sent telepathic commands inside my head, but the madman next to me continued.

"Welcome, welcome, Adam Shapiro. You are being *very* welcome in my store."

It would have been so much better if my father didn't speak *any* English.

"Aba, please stop talking to him," I hissed in Urdu. But my father was deaf to my pleas.

"Buy anything your heart is desiring, Adam. I am giving 11.5 percent discount to all of Mona's friends. Luckily she doesn't have many, does she? Ha. Ha."

Adam frowned in confusion or possibly revulsion and nodded. Then he wandered away from us. Down the snack aisle. Grabbed a large bag of ketchup chips and a four-pack of iced tea and came to the counter. "Please don't speak to him again, Aba." I tried again. Then I came upon what I thought was a genius idea and whispered in Urdu, "He only speaks French, Aba."

But to my father I did not exist. Only the exalted Customer existed. He smiled at Adam. I could hear the wheels in my father's brain turning as he stared at him.

Aba wriggled his head from side to side. "*Bon choor. Kom mint tallay vu?*" I turned to stone. Adam froze. Neither of us was sure which language my father was attempting. Taking the silence as encouragement, Aba continued, "I am new to your country, Adam. I am seeing in your eyes you are intellectual boy. Knowing English *and* French? Shabaash. No passing your time smoking the tam pon, na. Stay A-plus, boy, okay? With your discount the total is being three twenty-nine." I died a thousand agonizing deaths with every word my father uttered.

Adam had the decency to:

1. Ignore me completely;
2. Look my father in the eye, smile, say thank you and walk out.

WHY, ALLAH, WHY???? I HAVE BEEN BAD, BUT NOT *THIS* BAD.

CHAPTER TWELVE

December

Sunday, December 1, 1991

1:24 a.m. DEAR ALLAH, THANK YOU FOR OUR PERFECT LITTLE BABY BROTHER!

After having painful contractions late last night, Ami went into the hospital while Tutoo went over to Mrs. Rousopoulos's for the night. I came home from the gas station and went straight to bed. Aba rushed to the hospital. Ami and Aba came home a few hours later, and I got some precious moments with my baby brother without Tutoo around. Eventually Tutoo walked over from Mrs. Rousopoulos's, and we took turns holding our baby brother in our laps. Aba took about a gazillion pictures!

We can't stop staring at his little baby toes and little baby fingers! Each yawn and each stretch is the most precious movement by any creature in the history of humankind *EVER*!

He smells like butter and milk and heaven and sugar.

Monday, December 2, 1991

Ami and Aba can't decide on a name for him, so they've asked Tutoo and me for ideas.

Since Tutoo is super into animals, she wants to name him "lion." The Urdu and Arabic word for lion is *osama*, which is the perfect name for the only boy in the Hasan family. His little cries sound like tiny roars anyway! So *Osama Mohammed Hasan* it is! Oh, Allah, what a bright future awaits him with such an auspicious name!

We'll call him Sama for short. Ami let us rock him to sleep today and we were even allowed to change his tiny little nappies!

Tuesday, December 3, 1991

He's such a cutie patootie!!

I love him so much!!!

Wednesday, December 4, 1991

He cries a bit if we don't rock him to sleep just so. Aww! Even his crying is cute!

Thursday, December 5, 1991

The crying went on a bit longer than seemed necessary.

Friday, December 6, 1991

Ami didn't change Sama's nappy last night. Aba picked him out of the crib and he was wet. His diaper had leaked through. So this was why he was up all night crying!

Aba took me aside after dinner:

"You're twelve now. From now on, you must help your mother with all the chores inside the house."

"But Aba, I have to prepare for school. I'm watching all this TV so my English can be A-one, and I can get the top marks at school and be better than everyone! Either I'm number one or I'm nothing. You understand, right?"

"Did you hear me? Help your mother out. She can't do all this work by herself. No one in this house lifts a finger. Wash some dishes. Make some rotis. How can she be expected to manage all this housework? From now on I want you in the kitchen doing the woman things." But Aba *also* wants me helping out at the gas station, so I guess it's the worst of both worlds for me!

Aba moved Sama's crib into my room and put me on diaper duty for the night. I also had to wash two pots and do a load of laundry. All the whites came out a light shade of pink, and I made sure to leave some gunk in each pot too.

I suppose it can't be that difficult to take care of a baby for one night, though. Every mother since the time of Muhammad has done this, right? Just feed and burp. What could go wrong?

Later that night and into Saturday, December 7, 1991

10:00 p.m. Osama's tiny roars not so tiny.

11:00 p.m. Those tiny little nappies sure can hold quite a lot of . . . excrement.

1:00 a.m. Sama might have gas.

1:30 a.m. Needs another burp maybe.

1:32 a.m. He probably needs some cuddling.

1:45 a.m. Some pacing around the apartment.

2:22 a.m. He might be hot. Switching him to a cotton onesie.

2:24 a.m. Might be cold. Blanket back on.

2:34 a.m. If I keep my hand on his back just *so* . . .

2:48 a.m. Swaddling is *THE* answer.

3:01 a.m. *Was* the answer for forty-five seconds.

3:03 a.m. He likes it when I walk him up and down the hallway.

3:46 a.m. My back is on fire—walked him back and forth until I thought my legs were going to buckle! Woke Tutoo up. Her turn to pace with demon brother up and down the hallway. My eardrums are ringing from all this racket.

3:47 a.m. Definitely not having any children of my own. I'm going to adopt them at the age they stop crying.

Sunday, December 8, 1991

Early morning. The little booger finally slept for five hours straight. I fell asleep on the floor next to him in a pile of my own drool. He woke up squealing like a kitten and gave me a daft gummy smile. "Gah." He dribbled and kicked his pudgy feet at me, then he held on to my pinky finger dead tight. I suppose taking care of him here and there might not be the worst thing on earth.

Monday, December 9, 1991

What does Aba do during the day? Does he even send out résumés? At home he's always lounging on the sofa watching TV in his white cotton tee and loose underwear. The job-wallahs could call anytime now. Shouldn't he put on a button-down shirt and tie? Shouldn't his briefcase be packed and ready by the door, *just in case?*

In even WORSE news, it's been a FULL NINE DAYS since Adam walked into Aba's store last Saturday. I've been too mortified to talk to him after that day, and he has not approached me either! Is the torrid love affair that I'd envisioned between us over before it even began?!

The agony.

Tuesday, December 10, 1991

Ms. Rousopoulos signed Ami and herself up for a free course at the Woodlawn Public Library on Wednesday evenings from seven to nine. Tutoo and I found the flyer tacked to the fridge—

SIGN UP FOR AN 8-WEEK COURSE ON
MEMOIR WRITING
LEARN HOW TO MAKE YOUR JOYS &
SORROWS NAIL-BITING!

Tomorrow is their first class and Ami is buzzing with excitement. Guess who is going to be stuck watching Sama and Sofia while the mothers are busy doodling their memories? Yes, You guessed right! It is Tutoo and me! How selfish of both these mothers, Allah! Shouldn't being a mother be the lone focus of their lives? Why would they *also* want to do anything else? Why aren't we enough, Allah?

Wednesday, December 11, 1991

The parents are fighting again. Ami went to her memoir-writing class tonight. At the door, Aba told her writing doesn't pay the bills. Ami told him to stuff it. Aba muttered, "Where?" under his breath. Then he came inside and slumped in front of the TV. I bet he's wondering why he's not enough either.

As I get older, I see now that life is difficult and exhausting and sad. The painful things in life:

1. TV stations with long-winded nature documentaries.
2. Fathers with long-winded facts on nature.
3. Crushes who don't send you love poems.
4. Crushes who don't talk to you.
5. Crushes who have forgotten you exist.

Thursday, December 12, 1991

Another day. Another argument between Ami and Aba. Ami moved Aba's favorite Bic pen from its position by the telephone. Aba complained about how he was supposed to write down details about his interviews (that are sure to happen any day now) if Ami kept arranging and rearranging all the stationery in the place? Aba huffed and puffed about how difficult Ami made his daily life by moving his stationery and how she was sabotaging his job prospects, then settled down in the middle of the sofa with the TV remote and noisily changed channels.

Ami stormed into her bedroom, shutting the door with a bang, then stormed out a minute later holding three ball-point pens that she slammed onto the coffee table in front of Aba, telling him to "stuff them where the sun don't shine." Tutoo and I clapped our hands over our mouths to stop ourselves from laughing—there are any number of places on Aba's body that this could be!!

I had never noticed my mother's short fuse and my father's tiresome tirades before. What a terrible match they are, Allah! Did they always dislike each other this much?

Friday, December 13, 1991

I've missed the last two basketball games since Sama was born, and Coach McLean was nice enough not to penalize me for it, but I have promised to be there for the last two games this month!

This weekend, we're playing against Cole Harbour Junior High. They've *also* lost most of their games for the past six years, which means that there's a slim, but not non-existent chance we could win against them! A win would boost our incredibly low morale.

Saturday, December 14, 1991

Ross and Sherry dropped by the gas station today. Aba told me to go hang out with my friends for a bit because he couldn't do the numbers properly with me around. So I left with my friends and went around the corner to have a local Dartmouth delicacy—the donair, or shawarma. "Delicious Dartmouth Donairs" is Mr. Baliki's new business. Isn't it nice that this was a local delicacy back in Dubai too?

This world is pretty complicated, isn't it, Allah? How strange that everything and everyone is so magically, wonderfully complicated and messy and layered and interconnected. That there's a bit of *that* and a bit of *this* in this great big world and that we're all jumbled up on the inside. "Our labels tell such a small part of our stories," Ross said sagely as the tahini sauce dribbled down his favorite fisherman's sweater.

Sunday, December 15, 1991

The Cole Harbour girls were beasts. We lost 51–31. In the locker room, Sherry snapped a towel at me. "Por qué you no give me the ball? Pass to me, Mona. Pass."

I shrugged. If I pass the ball, I know exactly what she'll do. She'll score and she'll get all the glory. I need to hold on to the ball and score for myself. That's how I'll win.

Monday, December 16, 1991

ADAM
INVITED
ME
TO
THE
WINTER
DANCE!!!!
(Well, okay, maybe-kinda-sort of.)

In math class, he turned around and asked, real casual, "You going to the Winter Dance in two days?" My heart jumped out of my chest but I kept it casual. "Maybe," I responded, super nonchalant.

"You should," he said and turned back toward the front.

!!!!!!!!!!!!!!!!!!!!!!!!!

Do I need him to spell it out in large lettering across the sky? NO, NOT I! Lo! And hark! Be it but a whisper, my heart hears you, my Dreamboat!

Tuesday, December 17, 1991

8:00 a.m. Lying down dead does not work. The parents don't want me to go to the dance because the schools they went to never had dances, and there are no grades or scholarships given out at dances, so what's the point really.

8:00 p.m. Struck a deal with the parentals. I promised to work the early Sunday shifts for the rest of the school year if I can go to the Winter Dance. The fools folded easily!

Wednesday, December 18, 1991

The school dance took place during the lunch hour in the gymnasium. I was hoping for nefarious lighting and scandalous music, but instead the gymnasium was brightly lit, and sickly sweet, saccharine music blared from the speakers.

Everyone was awkwardly grouped in twos and threes in the farthest corners they could find. Proving the rumors wrong, Keesha Beals was there with Sam. They were holding hands and sucking face, but he came up for air long enough to give me a welcoming wave hello and a genuine friendly smile, which proves that some princesses can perform miracles after all.

Adam walked in with two friends, and Ross rushed over to tell them the sob story about how I've never been to a school dance before, which made Adam come over and pull me onto the dance floor!!

"Imagine" came on and it seemed like the lights dimmed. Suddenly Adam's eyes were the only things in the room.

While I slow-danced at my first-ever dance with my Dreamboat, I knew that this was a Very Special Moment. It was an Opening in my one little life! I know openings are tiny. Minuscule. There's barely enough space for a razor-thin beam of light. But you have to reach out and grab those moments when you see them, even though you're scared shitless. You just have to be hopeful and a little bit reckless. I knew that either in this moment, here and now, this boy was going to be mine or I was going to lose him forever. Adam smiled and mouthed the lyrics to the song and his cheeks burst into red patches. Now I *knew* for triple-sure that this was indeed my Moment!

I closed my eyes and leaned in. Our lips parted. The kiss was sloppy and wet and messy and wonderful. For the briefest of seconds, this crazy world stopped pulling and pushing, spinning and whirling, and I felt it. I was no longer on stationary ground—I was flying. Out of my cocoon and into a brand-new world.

Thursday, December 19, 1991

Math was the first class of the day. Adam turned around and shrugged. "If it's cool with you, I might call you, yeah." Everything about him is so smooth and relaxed. Doesn't he know that every time I see him, butterflies are battling it out in my insides? But I played it ICY *COOOOOOOL*, like Nova Scotian freezing rain. "Yeah, sure, I mean, I guess if you want to. I mean I'd like you to, but if you don't, whatever. I won't be waiting by the phone all hot and sweaty and uncool or anything. Call or don't call but yeah, okay, call me okay, please." I wrote down the number for the gas station inside his math textbook.

Friday, December 20, 1991

Last day of school before the winter holidays!

Mr. D. reminded us about our hero assignment. He wants it turned in the first day back after holidays! In between working at the gas station and my chores at home and caring for Sama and making sure Adam ~~falls~~ stays madly in love with me, when am I ever going to find time to do it?

266

I can't think about how much I need to do. I can only just dive in and do. One obstacle at a time. This weekend, I need to focus on the fact that we have a Big Game on Sunday!

Sunday, December 22, 1991

LAST GAME OF THE YEAR!

Today we were up against a team from the big city—the Halifax Junior High Thundercats! It was an away game so we had to meet at their school at 7:00 a.m. sharp. I jumped out of bed at 5:00 a.m. Ami had been up with Sama all night but she got up early, watched me load up on carbs and smiled at me wryly. "Once upon a time, I used to play cricket with my cousins. It was in the back gulleys of Islamabad." Why are parents always yammering on and on about their glory days? I nodded politely anyway. "I'm proud of you," she said and turned away. Before she could leave the room, I threw my arms around her. We have our moments, Allah.

Ami drove me to the school quietly and dropped me off in the parking lot. The girls from my team were huddled together shivering and stamping their feet. Because we were playing girls from the big city our team was a bundle of nerves. Coach McLean gave us a pep talk in the parking lot, her words coming out in a misty cloud. "Every new day is a blank slate, girls—donna forget that and donna let anyone evar convince yah otherwise. Light that fire in yah belly. Yah have to *want* to fly."

Okay, let me start with the stats:

Mona—14 points and 7 rebounds. 1 steal. No blocks.

Sherry—21 points and 16 rebounds. 5 steals. 3 blocks.

Sherry was on fire! She had six 3s!! That's the second-most 3s in a single game in our school history! The Halifax Thundercats started strong in the first quarter and took a 14–8 lead, but us Dartmouth girls came roaring into the second quarter, and by the third quarter we had a 5-point lead. We stayed strong on the defense and by fourth quarter, the score remained close. With only 5:15 remaining in the game, the Thundercats moved in on us. They took the lead at 45–42. Then Sherry did it—she landed another 3. Suddenly we were tied and went into overtime!

With only thirteen seconds left on the clock at overtime, I made my first and only steal and passed to Sherry.

13

12

11

10

9

8

7

6

5

4

Sherry turned. She twirled. She blocked and she advanced. No, she RUMBLED! The energy in the gymnasium was electric. Every player was buzzing with a desire to win! With only three seconds left on the overtime clock, Sherry scored her sixth 3-pointer and everyone leaped off the bleachers and rushed the floor! This was it! We'd won our first-ever game in nine years!! There was so much cheering and screaming and hooting and clapping, I thought I might lose my hearing.

No one from my family was there to see it. Aba was at the store. Ami had to be home with Sama. Tutoo was helping with chores. But you know what, Allah, the victory still tasted as sweet. I guess you don't always need an audience. Winning really isn't for impressing anyone else. The real victories in life hit you somewhere deep inside. In the places no one can see.

And yeah, Sherry got that winning shot. But it took all of us to work at it together. Supporting each other. Teamwork. And that sisterhood thing, I guess.

Tuesday, December 24, 1991

Phone call from Adam!

We talked about his obnoxious older brother, his workaholic father and his favorite book. I am embarrassed to tell you, Allah, but he told me it was *The Little Prince*! The first order of business will be introducing him to quality literature fit for his age bracket! I went on and on about my favorite book—*The Secret Diary of Adrian Mole, Aged 13¾*, which Hala had gifted me in Dubai. I told him it's about a young boy in a faraway place called England and that *my* favorite books were the ones that were portals into different lives and different worlds. In a voice that told me he was smiling, Adam told me to stop yammering on and on about it and promised to give it a read.

He let me know that he thinks the winter holidays are a total SNOOZE-FEST too, and he can't wait for school to start up again. He likes doing homework and acing all his tests as well!!!!

Later that evening, when I was home, I thought about my homework assignment from Mr. D. and cornered Ami.

"Ami, are you ever going to be okay? Why do you sleep all day?"

"What do you need, Mona?"

"I need help to write an essay for school. Mr. D. told us to find a hero and write about that. I need your help."

"I don't know anything about Canadian heroes."

"If I pick someone Canadian, Mr. D. will say I cheated again. I need a hero from another world. Any heroes you know from Pakistan?"

"The British didn't teach us about our heroes."

"Hmm ... what if we wrote that you're my hero?"

"Women can be heroes in your essay?"

"Why not? Then for sure he'll know I didn't cheat! Ever do anything hero-like? Save someone from a burning building? Or ... something?"

"Oh Mona, I don't know."

"Come on. I can't write this alone. Think. Didn't you do anything exciting in your life? Something adventurous?"

"Well, my life was a *bit* interesting, maybe. Your grandfather was an ambassador for many years, you know. It caused some headaches with politics for us later on, but I did get to grow up all over India, and I even lived for a few years in Indonesia."

"I never knew that!"

"Indonesia has flowers the size of small babies. And they have trees where the bark looks like a watercolor painting. It's a beautiful country. The food is just out-of-this-world extraordinary, and I can still speak a little of the language. And you know, I used to keep a diary just like you."

"You did?"

"Yes. And your Aba used to be considered very handsome once. He came from a poor family but I knew he was going places, so I took a chance on him. We weren't supposed to get married."

"You weren't?"

"No, it was very scandalous doing what we did at that time. His parents, Dada and Dadi, were very angry with us at first, and I guess my parents, your Nanijaan and Nanajaan, are still angry."

"Really?"

"Yes."

"Ami this is all great stuff! Tell me more about your time in Indonesia and the year you met Aba."

Tutoo sidled over and we both listened to stories from my mother that we'd never heard in their entirety before. In the end, I'm not sure that I will use any of it for my assignment after all, but asking my mother about her life made Ami sit up a little straighter and even look a little younger.

"Hmm, I guess I've been a bit of a warrior in my own life, haven't I? I've overcome some difficulties before and maybe I can overcome them again," she mused to herself.

What was most surprising was that all this time, my mother was living right next to Tutoo and me, and we had no idea that she was this interesting!

Wednesday, December 25, 1991

It's the birth of Prophet Eesa (they call him Jesus here), and Canadian Christians have gone crazy with their commemoration! For weeks now, all the stores have been playing Christmas jingles. Ms. Rousopoulos promised us that the music will stop after today.

Tutoo invited Sofia and Ms. Rousopoulos over for our potluck Christmas lunch, and I invited Sherry and her family. Since we don't have that many chairs, we pushed the sofa and coffee table out of the way and put bedsheets on the living room floor. We all sat cross-legged on the floor and passed dishes around. Sherry and her family brought a mountain of pupusas, a large pot of fish soup, and a seed drink called horchata that Sherry's mom had been up all night brewing. We placed these dishes next to Ami's pakoras and biryani and raita, and Ms. Rousopoulos's moussaka and spanakopita and honey cake. We spoke in broken English so everyone could understand, and laughed good-naturedly at our own and each other's mispronunciations. Who knew that food tastes that much better and laughter is that much deeper when they're shared with those going through similar struggles?

Even Aba took a break from the gas station to join us.

After the main dishes, Ami and Ms. Rousopoulos recited a page each from their memoirs. Ms. Rousopoulos bored all of us by sharing a story of making wooden birdhouses with her grandfather as a child in Greece, and Ami bored all of us with a poem about her playing gully cricket with her brothers. Sherry's family politely clapped after each reading and looked at each other with big eyes.

When it came time for presents, Aba said he had a present for Tutoo and me and carried in a large box with holes at the top. He set the box down tenderly in the middle of the room. Sherry's mother jumped when she heard the mewling. Aba explained that the local shelter gives out orphaned kittens for free.

She was a tiny little thing. Her coat was a velvety black and the toes on her back legs were white. Part of her left ear was missing. Despite whatever she had been through, she was still playful and joyous. Ready to lunge at this world with reckless abandon and faith. Second to my little sister and brother, she's the most beautiful creature I've ever seen. Tutoo and I named her Mushkil, which is the Urdu word for difficulty or hardship, because Tutoo and I both agreed that mushkil isn't always a bad thing—sometimes it gives you an opportunity to grow wings.

Mushkil amused us by licking our toes and then scampered up to greet Pierre Trudeau, who seemed to understand the threat as he then swam fast circles in his goldfish bowl.

Who knew that something free would bring so much joy?

(Actually I guess maybe I did have a clue.)

Thursday, December 26, 1991

Mushkil slept at my feet last night. Tutoo was dead jealous. Technically the cat belongs to both of us.

Friday, December 27, 1991

The weather has taken a turn for the worse. There was a huge dump of that dreaded white monstrosity last night, and it's made driving slippery and hazardous today. It doesn't seem possible that we had a jolly get-together just two days ago. Aba came home from the gas station in a foul mood—he complained that the dal was overcooked and the rice was soggy. When will this deep freeze ever end?

Saturday, December 28, 1991

Minus thirty-eight today. There was a weather advisory on the news. Public transportation was closed but the city kept all the roads open. Aba and I sat at the gas station waiting for the beleaguered masses who might need to fuel up.

How many people can say that they've felt both plus thirty-eight and minus thirty-eight in one year? For the record, one isn't better than the other—they both SUCK. Equally.

$+38 = -38$

No customer actually came inside. They all did full-serve, so I balanced the accounts, stacked coins into their tubes and stretched out inventory duties while Aba did the pumping. Through the dirty window, I watched my father pumping gas for customers in the middle of a snowstorm. The wind whipped around him, throwing snow into his eyes and down his neck. He staggered from pump to car with a daft smile plastered on his face. There was no scarf around his neck. He didn't even pull up his collar. And no gloves! Why could this man not keep his gloves on?! He left them on the counter each time he rushed out to pump gas.

After filling up gas for each customer, Aba walked back into the store with dry, chapped hands. His customer-greeting face morphed into morose-father face, and he sat grumpily in a corner rubbing his palms and blowing on his popsicle fingers. When I stared too long, he scowled. "So are you getting A-pluses or what?"

I didn't answer him. We sat in sullen silence during our shift and also during our drive home.

Does my father actually believe that I owe him now? That my grades have to atone for his sacrifice? That I'll resignedly follow the career path he chooses? Marry the man he picks?

Daft man. He needs to keep his gloves on.

Sunday, December 29, 1991

Finally warming up a little, which means it's a balmy minus ten today. I think I may even have seen one of the European-Canadians out and about in shorts and a T-shirt.

Phone call from Adam, who told me that Cowtown, or Calgary, gets even colder! I can't even fathom what *colder* would feel like.

Monday, December 30, 1991

Right before bed, I remembered the assignment from Mr. D.'s class—it was crumpled in a ball at the bottom of my backpack. It's due the first day back from holidays, so I'd better get started! Gulp.

BACKGROUND: *A hero is someone we look up to or admire because of their outstanding qualities or achievements. A hero* can be someone close to us, such as a relative, friend or neighbor. Or it may be someone famous, whose stories of struggle inspire us: an athlete, an actor, a musician or an artist. Discussions about "heroes" are constant themes in history and literature, and a subject that we will cover extensively this upcoming year.

PURPOSE: In this assignment, I want you to think about some heroes that you know personally. Provide clear reasons for choosing their particular acts as examples of heroism. In your last paragraph, present an individual you consider to be **your** primary guiding hero in life. After writing the assignment, you will then use the information you gathered to work in a group setting and create a presentation to the class on your combined discoveries about what heroism is.

AUDIENCE: You are writing this for yourself, but remember that this essay will also be shared with your selected group.

FORM: Write a one-page essay. Ensure that you answer the following questions in your essay: (1) What is a definition of a hero? (2) What are the extraordinary qualities of a hero? (3) Who is the primary guiding hero in your life and why did you select them?

DUE: First Day of Class, 1992 ~ worth 30% of your final grade

Tuesday, December 31, 1991

I woke up early. Sat at my desk and typed out my assignment for Mr. D. on Aba's electronic typewriter.

"THE HERO ASSIGNMENT"
by Mona Hasan, 12 years old

Heroes are people who perform great deeds of bravery. They help others even if they might get hurt or die, like firefighters who rush into burning buildings to pull out the trapped people inside. Heroes are strong and powerful people who use their strength to help others. Ripley in the movie *Aliens* was one such hero. But off the screen and in real life, heroes are usually ordinary people fighting against extraordinary circumstances. Often appearing meek and mild, their superpower is resilience.

I've met many such heroes. They open gymnasiums for girls, smuggle books, experiment with the length and color of their tights, love who their heart tells them to. They stand up for others. Live in languages that they are still learning. They start over. Begin again. Love again. Trust again. Heroes always rise, undaunted. It's in their rising that they are made. Their stories of struggle and strength don't make it into our newspapers but maybe they should. Perhaps alongside reading the headlines of everything happening in the world, we also need to read about and remind ourselves of the extraordinary lives being lived by ordinary people every single day. Lives full of hope, humor, bravery and kindness.

Even though I've met many great heroes, the primary guiding hero of my life that I'd like to present is myself, Mona Hasan. Fully twelve years old as of two months ago. I'm a hero too. It's taken me a while to understand this truth. I'm my own hero because I question the world around me and dream of a better one.

I bet that each and every one of us has a story of struggle and of hope, and that in our lives, each and every one of us has been or will be our own hero. Look out World, here comes Mona Hasan, twelve and nine weeks.

Acknowledgments

First and foremost, I would like to thank my wonderful agent, Amy Tompkins, who swooped in like a fairy godmother at just the right moment, sprinkled her fairy dust, waved her magic wand and this manuscript became a book. The impact of her enthusiasm and encouragement for my manuscript cannot be overstated—it meant the world, made all the difference, and here we are.

Equally, I wish to thank my editor extraordinaire, Lynne Missen. Lynne guided this manuscript to become immeasurably and immensely better, and I am indebted to her detailed, constructive feedback. Thank you, Lynne! There is a great team of people at Tundra who made this book possible and I am so grateful for their efforts: Peter Phillips, for his meticulous eye and attention to detail, and Yash Kesanakurthy (former publishing assistant at PRHC), for championing the book in its early stage. I would also like to mention and thank Sarah Howden and Linda Pruessen for their contributions.

Additionally, I wish to signal out Sam Devotta and Vikki VanSickle for the exceptional work they do in promoting books and authors. A special shout out to the illustrator, Jameela Wahlgren, for capturing the tone and personality of this character in a beautiful cover.

I also wish to thank the extraordinary teachers and mentors that I've had the good fortune of encountering over the years. They created worlds out of words and inspired me to do the same: Aritha van Herk, Aruna Srivastava, Shaobo Xie, Nathalie Younglai, John May, Olive Senior, Martha Sepulveda, Tanaz Bhathena, Noor Naga and Cary Fagan. Thank you! Among this group of exceptionally generous teachers, I would like to single out Noor Naga for her guidance, comments and assistance on this manuscript.

I also wish to thank a small group of outstanding writers who were part of my writing group and support system for the completion of this manuscript. In this core group that met monthly, I shared early drafts and brainstormed voice, plot and themes. They are fellow writers and artists who gave of their time and energy tirelessly and generously: Anthony Chong, Basil Coward and Erinn Banting. Their feedback and support was invaluable and to them I owe everything (except the royalties, of course). Other writers who made priceless contributions: Fiona R. Clarke and Arlene Jacob. A special thank-you to my funny and ferociously intelligent cousin, Fahd. As well, to my sensitive and beautiful nieces, Zara E. and Ayana M. My world is richer for your feedback and for your friendship.

Thank you to the Ontario Arts Council and to Diaspora Dialogues, as well as Artscape Gibraltor.

I also wish to thank the most exceptional trio of human beings that have put up with me since my early twenties and refuse to let me go or let me down: Christine Cheung, Moortaza Bhaiji and Dalia Nagati. Since moving to Toronto, I have somehow managed to hoodwink others into life-long friendships: Onder Deligoz, Maria-Helena Moviglia, Amethyst Megaffin, Michelle Forrieter, Janet Fry, Samira Ahmed, Sara Ahmed, Bhargavi Varma, Suchi Garg and Tanya Methiwalla. So grateful that you are on this roller-coaster with me.

Love to my Harbourfront family—no longer an elevator ride away but forever in my heart. And to the best neighbors on this planet, the Flagwallahs—you are all truly amazing and I appreciate each and every one of you.

Immense gratitude to Dr. Gelareh Zadeh and nurse Christine Wong—fellow immigrants and superheroes in white coats, as well as to the other staff, nurses and residents at Toronto Western.

To my parents—Shireen and Haider, and to my siblings, Nimra, Nadia and Mohammed Ali—I would not be who I am without you. To Saif—I would not be where I am without you. Thank you for the love, laughter and support. Onwards and upwards.